ROAR

finding your strength,
within.

For further information and any questions visit our
Website www.businessinheels.com
Email info@businessinheels.com

ISBN: 978-0-6451639-1-9 (paperback)

Typeset & design by Karinya Kreations, Design Studio
www.kkreations.design

Cover art by Justine Martin

Edited by Steve Sweeney

Compiled, produced, and published by
Business in Heels International Pty Ltd

Acknowledgement

My heartfelt thanks go to Irene and Carole for their time and patience in reading the manuscript and for their constructive comments that played a significant part in shaping the finished work. Without your encouraging remarks, this manuscript might well have ended up in a drawer and never to see the light of day again.

As usual, thanks again Tom for applying your special magic to create the cover from my rambling synopsis of the story and vague ideas about art work.

And to Doug for his support and perseverance all through the creation of the first draft, which on this occasion took so long it was akin to gestating and elephant.

Words don't come close to expressing my appreciation.

About the Author

KAYLA DANOLI spent her early years traipsing around Australia and then Europe with her parents, and then completed her tertiary education in England before returning to Australia. There were a variety of jobs in various parts of Queensland before eventually making her way towards the coast. She now lives in a small coastal town on the Queensland coast where she works part-time on a charter vessel.

In the early days after settling in that small town, to fill in her spare time, both when at home and while on cruises, she started scribbling down her ideas for stories. These days, she writes whenever time permits. Her *Harbour Plaza* series, previously released in 2015 as monthly eBook episodes, was updated, extended and released in 2016 as the *Harbour Plaza: built on dreams* compilation. *Revenge is not Enough,* also released in 2016, was her first full-length novel.

A Life of Tea and Sugar is Kayla's tenth full-length novel.

Discover more about Kayla and her work by visiting
www.eaglemountbooks.com.au/kayla-danoli

or contact her at
admin@eaglemountbooks.com.au

Contents

Foreword
by Lisa Sweeney

Too often, women are expected to hold it in. Put a lid on it. Cork it. They're expected to turn the other cheek. Be demure. Sit still, look pretty.

But that just doesn't gel with all of us because we've got stories to tell and the world needs to hear them. We've got valuable contributions to make about life, work, love, children, marriage, chasing your dreams, building a business, escaping tyranny, being the best mother we can be, dealing with diseases that aren't our fault and getting back on a steady course.

We know that reading others' stories can serve as our own reference point, a fork in the road, a chance to say, "Enough is enough!" We know that the spark for another woman to reset her destiny can come from a sentence, a phrase or a word that resonates in someone else's story. Stories promote action like no other form of communication and have been used to educate and inspire humans from the time we came down from the trees.

The brave women who have penned their stories in this anthology have put their hearts and souls on the line. They have recognised their own failings and formidable features and laid them out for others to learn from. For some it stung to put the words down. Memories were dragged up from the past that were terrible then and only just bearable now. For others it's been cathartic, like an awakening has occurred as their fingers danced over the keyboard and the words appeared in front of them on their screens. And for others...

"OMG... am I really going to let the world read that?!?!"

These nine courageous women have gone out of their way to tell it like it is. Prepare to be shocked, to cry, to admire their bravery. Prepare to shake your head in disbelief. Whatever your reaction, know that these women are no longer prepared to cork it, sit still and look pretty.

Prepare to hear them ROAR.

The Business in Heels Team hopes you enjoy ROAR,

Lisa Sweeney

Job title ⎬ CEO, Business in Heels International Pty Ltd

Website ⎬ www.businessinheels.com

Chrissie Stobbs

Chrissie is passionate about supporting others to take control of their situation and to live fully with purpose and clarity. After a wonderful career managing Corporate Travel offices in London, she recognised the 'burn-out' signs and shifted her focus to train as a Reflexologist. This fulfilled her natural inclination to support others dealing with stress in their life in a nurturing, relaxing environment.

Chrissie first became curious to learn how our unconscious mind works to help process personal challenges that arose after her son's diagnosis with Duchenne Muscular Dystrophy - a degenerative condition with no cure.

This news threw her family onto a new path, dramatically different to the one they had planned. Trying to deal with overwhelming emotions of anger, sadness and guilt, she felt lost, confused and stuck, anchored to the pain for some time. Chrissie sought strategies to cope, focus and move forward and as a result began studying various therapies. Realising how powerful these techniques are, and with a desire to help others take control of their emotional well-being, Chrissie completed further studies including her Diploma of NLP & Hypnotherapy and became a certified trainer.

Bringing both her personal experience and these modalities together, Chrissie offers a coaching frame-work to support those wanting to release emotions lingering from past events and move into a future they desire. Chrissie's vision to empower others to live life on purpose continues to expand through offering personal coaching, corporate workshops, and co-founding The Collective Coaching Academy to train and certify others with these amazing tools and 'increase the ripple effect of change in the world'.

Website	ccanlp.com/chrissie
Email	chrissie@yourbodyandsole.com
Facebook	facebook.com/yourmindbodysole
Instagram	instagram.com/yourmindbodysole
LinkedIn	linkedin.com/in/chrissie-stobbs
Degrees	Dip. Neuro-Linguistic Programming (NLP) / Dip. Hypnotherapy / Dip. Reflexology
	Master Practitioner & Certified Trainer of Neuro-Linguistic Programming, Time Line Therapy®, Hypnotherapy, NLP Coaching
	EFT (Tapping) Practitioner / BBus.

ROAR

The **Scream**

Breathe.

The water gurgled down the drain. I should get out, but I couldn't move. I sat there hugging my knees, squeezed into our half-bath shower tub, staring at the white tiles. Numb. Confused. My husband had taken the boys out to give me some space and he'd run the bath in an attempt to calm the stress he could sense building behind my eyes.

But the panic kept rising in my chest like waves of an incoming tide, the intensity building with each breath. Eventually the screaming inside my head escaped. A guttural, primal sound exploded and reverberated around the tiny, tiled room – an outpouring of anger wrapped in sadness.

How could this be happening?...

The soft music and dimmed lighting were in stark contrast to the bright lights and chaos he was expecting. I had secretly upgraded us to Upper Class for our flight from London to Sydney and even the champagne glasses appeared to be clinking in applause as the hostess guided us 'left', past the bar towards our seats. Ricky's face was priceless. Instead of squishing his 6-foot self into the teeny seat he was expecting for our flight across the world, we were guided to the flatbed seats adorned with fancy toiletries, pyjamas, and menus. He was speechless as the hostess offered the wine list and booked us a mid-flight massage. Ah yes, this was how travel should be done, I was blissfully happy as we took off on another adventure, dreaming and planning our future life together.

Oh... how I LOVED my job in corporate travel! After leaving New Zealand in my early twenties I embraced '*the world is my oyster*' attitude my parents had instilled in me and had many exciting escapades around the globe. With the hindsight only maturity brings, I realise how incredibly lucky I was to have experienced over a decade living in London working with wonderful people in a company that was booming and where the '*work hard, play hard*' ethos was in full force.

On top of the great job, awesome friends, weekends spent clubbing or jetting off somewhere fabulous like Iceland or Italy, I met Ricky in 2005. The cliché continued with a *love at first sight* story. Inseparable since we met, relocating to Sydney's Northern Beaches and having two children, we were ridiculously happy and loving life by the beach, everything was just so damn perfect.

Until it wasn't...

When the paediatrician rang, it was *days* earlier than expected and my alarm bells were ringing. He instructed me to gather both children and Ricky and meet him at his office immediately.

While the assistant fussed over the boys, Ricky and I entered the office. I noted the visitor chairs were positioned to the side of the broad desk, closer to the doctor's chair. "That's a little dramatic", I thought. But as he sat with tears in his eyes, he delivered the words; "DNA, diagnosis, degenerative, Duchenne." The air suddenly felt thick, my mind went numb. Ricky's hand squeezed mine, I shut my eyes and we discovered why Zachy had been falling frequently and was unable to climb stairs. We discovered that over time, because of his type of muscular dystrophy, he would lose the ability to walk, to breathe on his own and to live. We discovered all this as he sat outside the door rolling Lightning McQueen across the floor with his brother. Our perfect world shifted beneath our feet and a wrenching pain settled in our chests.

Breathe. Don't talk. Stay calm.

We drove home in pelting rain. Each *swish* of the wipers seemingly clearing away the tears that were threatening to escape any second.

Breathe. Don't cry. Not yet.

We carried Zachy up the stairs like we'd done a hundred times before, only now knowing why he struggled to climb them himself. We were struck by the realisation he would *never* run and chase his brother up or down or, well... anywhere. Words kept thumping around my head; "wheelchair at primary school, short life expectancy, no, there's no cure." It was a jumbled mess I couldn't untangle. As we returned to our apartment, we were confronted by

by Chrissie Stobbs

boxes for our upcoming move to suburban Victoria. This new, monumental shift to our life path crashed through my soul and I began to break.

Ricky saw the cracks appearing, ran my bath and took the boys out. Desperation and fear triggered an avalanche of emotion deep within. An angry voice emerged inside my head, fuelled by the confusion. "What have you done? You made him. You *broke* him. He will hate you. Will Ricky blame you? *I blame you!*" And so began my journey down this slippery slope of intense guilt and self-loathing. The walls of perfection were tumbling down. Once adorned with dreams of travel and adventures, these were washed away with my tears into the cold water and down the drain as I finally pulled the plug. I no longer knew what the future held and felt completely lost. Anguish rolled itself into a ball the size of my fist and settled into a new home in my chest. I thought there would have been some relief after the scream. It only served to lock it in.

Life got busy – only weeks earlier we decided to relocate 1,000km south to a growing locality near the Great Ocean Road in Victoria where comparable prices offered a house with a yard instead of a small apartment. Originally, leaving our friends suggested another adventure, but now, I saw the world through different eyes. With no support network at all, it felt daunting and overwhelming. Panic attacks started. Packing up and saying goodbye was painful this time.

Our new life in Victoria was frantic, Ricky frequently worked interstate and Zachy's condition now endlessly occupying my mind, I sacrificed sleep for late night internet scouring and put my own health lower on the priority list. I got lost in research papers and connected with other Duchenne families around the globe looking desperately for something, anything that could give our boy a better chance. I completely sabotaged any self-care habits as the vengeful voice that had arisen was adamant; "You don't deserve to be happy or healthy." Debilitating migraines were my body's signal to slow down but I was too busy to stop and listen.

A new town requires new connections, *everywhere*. Initially we thought, "Let's not tell anyone so he won't be treated differently." Well, this great plan failed on day one... at playgroup, I winced inside watching confident kids shove past Zachy up the ladder to the slide. They were impatient with his struggle and oblivious to their own strength and speed. Oh, how I didn't want to hover! But suddenly his weaknesses felt amplified, I found myself explaining what was happening to the other mums amongst a flood of tears I seemed unable to hold back. More tissues were offered as I sat in the new day-care centre explaining his needs and how the condition would progress. I learnt to take short shallow breaths to manage the tightness in my chest *every time* the word "Duchenne" rolled off my tongue. The scream haunted the depths of that pain, teasing the edges when my guard was down and threatening to escape in the middle of each conversation. I suppressed the urge, kept my head down and suffered through the internal echo instead. It was so deafening at times I wondered how others couldn't hear it.

Breathe, keep going.

Time rolled by, we did our best to get on with life and hold it together. It was as if I blinked, and months could pass by. Ironic because all I wanted to do was slow time down. Birthdays arrived and each extra candle brought more uncertainty of the challenges

by Chrissie Stobbs

the next year would bring. I knew I had to shift myself out of this darkness, I just wasn't sure how.

> "Sometimes you have to let go of the picture of what you thought life would be like and learn to find joy in the story you are actually living."
> Rachel Marie Martin

This quote in my newsfeed grabbed my attention, "*Ohhh, I like that!*" whispered a new internal voice. It was like finally opening a window after you'd 'battened down the hatches' during a long, heavy storm... I gave myself a nudge "*it's time to let the light in, enjoy the sunshine*". But was that easier said than done?

Then I met Sarah.

Sarah lost her beautiful baby before his second birthday. His life was taken by a virus with absolutely no warning. Just like that he was gone, overnight. Her experience had a profound impact on me. Since then, anytime I am struggling, I remind myself, "Zachy is still here, cuddling, laughing and falling asleep in my arms. *How lucky am I?*"

This was more than sunshine; this was a huge rainbow that guided me out of the darkness.

Recognising the shift this positive reflection created I purposefully began to seek every opportunity to feel appreciation for our life. Shortly after Zachy's birth I joined a Network Marketing company that had a wonderful impact on our health and created an income. When it's done properly, this business model can support families whilst providing flexibility to work around busy schedules, it truly allowed me to focus on both the boys through this time and I was surrounded by an uplifting community of people seeking to improve their lives. I was deeply grateful for all of this and the personal development that the company offered.

It was at a work conference the next rainbow appeared. Nick Vujicic's story was projected in surround sound to the audience. Listening to the challenges he faced I considered the dark moments he must have endured; I was inspired by his message to live a 'life without limits' despite having no arms or legs. I recognised his parents must have played a part in creating an environment for him to thrive and not live life as a victim of his circumstance.

"Right, so how the hell do I do that too?" This new voice within me was gaining traction.

But the biggest question remained. How could I do *anything* when this ball of anguish continued to harbour the scream? I was unable to squash my desire to release the sound to the outside world whenever I considered our situation. At the same conference I sobbed as our company raised funds for Make-A-Wish Foundation. My heart crushed as I realised 'we are one of those families now', we'd joined a club nobody wanted to be a part of.

Don't scream. Breathe.

Funny how when you focus on the sunshine, more rainbows appear. Shortly after a friend shared her experience of Neuro-Linguistic Programming (NLP) and Time Line Therapy®. She proposed it could release the grip of these emotions I continued to carry around and outlined the benefits from learning these techniques myself. "Could these really be the tools to help me move forward?" The hopeful voice got louder as I searched online for options.

Plans fell into place with curious ease. I soon found myself in a training room, balancing the workbook on my lap, open to learning and ready to change the trajectory of our life. I reflect with a sense of wonder now as I did not truly recognise then, the significant part this new training would play for my mindset, my attitude, my family and for others.

It was a personal journey at first. I learned to understand the workings of my unconscious mind, how to manage my emotional state and, amazingly, I was able to release all the emotional baggage I'd been carrying around. The anchor I had created with the bathroom scream scene was addressed, and the intensity of the pain disintegrated into acceptance… *FINALLY!*

I left feeling lighter, focused, and hopeful. I was ready to take on the world again.

Returning home with new skills and a fresh outlook, it was now my responsibility to instil a positive 'can-do' attitude and keep our family vibe high. Blessed with Ricky's willingness to come along for the ride, our relationship strengthened. Using my new positive mindset skills, we settled into a new pace of life. The lows still existed, but we honoured the space needed to navigate them and pulled each other up when required.

In my early London days, I studied Reiki and, whilst pregnant with Caleb, gained my Diploma of Reflexology with the vision to create a home-based business. Over the years, I'd kept my skills up-to-date and offered a mobile service but without any great consistency. As Zachy settled into his school routine, the opportunity to move into a beautiful, shared workspace arose. I was excited to help people relieve discomfort in their bodies and create balance in their lives. I continued studying higher levels of NLP, Time Line Therapy®, Hypnotherapy and EFT Tapping. It soon became apparent that, along with attending to my client's physical ailments, I had tools to help their emotional and mental well-being and relaunched my business as 'Your Mind, Body & Sole'.

This was truly a special time, everything felt aligned again. I'd found new purpose and Zachy was doing as well as could be expected, we focused on the present and started planning for new adventures.

Then... Covid.

The sweet spot of Zachy's life where we should be squeezing the juice out of each day, traveling and exploring whilst he still can with relative ease – nope, cancel that. Cancel *everything*. Weeks turned into months. My dream clinic closed. Kids were home schooled. Stormy clouds of uncertainty threatened as the entire world was thrust into a new era.

Breathe.

Instead of slipping down the path of helplessness and uncertainty again, I knew to stop focusing on closing doors. "Look for a new one to open, Chrissie, there is still much sunshine to be enjoyed."

Enduring months of Victorian 'lockdown' was certainly frustrating at times, but it also created plenty of quality time together. Board games emerged amidst the schoolwork and with Ricky working from home I utilised the time to study online. Hundreds of hours went into my Diploma and Trainer's qualifications and a chance pairing with another student led to a whole new world of possibilities. We shared a vision to help others consider their situation, understand their mindset, and take control of their lives. Born

by Chrissie Stobbs

from a desire to create a greater ripple effect than we could on our own, The Collective Coaching Academy quickly grew from an idea into a fantastic training company. Now we create graduates who can use their skills to uplift themselves, inspire their families and support others to release their emotional baggage and create the future they desire.

The world we live in continues to shift tremendously around us every day. I now enjoy relaxing in the bathtub and I no longer want to scream when I think or talk about Duchenne. Zachy is doing well considering his challenges, as he becomes more aware of his limitations we do our utmost to focus on what he *can* do. Dark clouds still roll in occasionally, we acknowledge this 'anticipatory grief'. When you grieve for what hasn't yet been lost, but know it will – it's like knowing a crash will happen and you can't stop it. It catches us on days when happiness should consume us like helping him dress up as a race car driver for '*What I want to be when I grow up*' day. We hold the space for this sadness but always let the sunshine through again, we look for ways to adapt and make life as fun as possible. I watch other families ahead of us on their Duchenne journey and realise time is ticking – but really, isn't this true for *all of us?*

> ## "We are not all in the same boat. We are in the same storm. Some of us are on super yachts. Some of us have just the one oar."
> Damian Barr

This metaphor resonates deeply with me. We are *all* sailing through a storm. It's more treacherous in some places, and we are *not* all in the same boat. Everyone is doing the best they can with the resources they have - some are sailing on super-yachts with support crew, others are battling to stay on course with torn sails or have lost an oar along the way. Some have fancy instruments to navigate the conditions while others are desperately bailing rising water from leaks below deck, and they hide their struggle from the world.

So amidst the day-to-day hustle of staying afloat, I encourage everyone to seek out the joy and possibilities in their lives. There is sunshine to be found behind those dark clouds and if you're having trouble finding it, seek out those that have travelled before you and can teach you how to adapt.

We don't always control what happens to us in this life, but we *can* choose how we respond. It is my hope that if you feel like you are sinking, or concealing your own internal scream, that you find the strength to stand up and wave for help. May we all learn to tie our boats together and share the resources required to get through the darker days and celebrate all the beautiful rainbows to be found on the other side.

"I went from thinking, "I can do this on my own and I will change the world" to feeling not good enough, not beautiful enough, not young enough, just not enough. I was shattered."

Michelle **Pavel**

With 60 just around the corner and so many women loking for or finding their purpose and stepping into their power after 50, I decided it was time for me to put my skills and talent to good use and start creating my own legacy.

Once we reach *our mature years* we can feel like it is too late to make something of ourselves, and often we aren't as confident as we were when we were young.

In my 40 year career I have been employed by, partnered with, owned, or contracted to over 60 small businesses, solopreneurs, or corporations in 20 different industries in office administration, design, technical writing, quality assurance, process management, marketing and so much more. At least half of that time, as a temp, I learned to gather relevant information, get up to speed quickly, and find out who my allies were. Being an introvert this was a bit of a challenge, but when I was young it didn't phase me as much as it did when I got older.

As I reached my older years I noticed I was smarter, more creative, more likely to get paid what I was worth, and more confident in so many ways. Yet I was also holding myself back from achieving my full potential, from shining my light, and from sharing my voice. I had my suspicions it was all related to trauma and limiting beliefs ,yet wasn't sure how to address those.

I immersed myself in personal and business development courses, became a course junkie, received so many potential opportunities, and discovered what I wanted for myself. Little by little, eventually finding my purpose to educate fempreneurs on the benefits of creating lucrative, authentic collaborations and partnerships that are in alignment with their values; without the fear of competition or judgement.

I also discovered that I love working with women who are also on a mission to achieve a bigger purpose to positively impact humanity, big or small. Whether that is creating their own tribe, supporting others to create their tribe, or innovating and sharing messages that change lives.

I hope my story inspires you to 'Make It Happen' - whatever that looks like for you!

To connect with me, share your story, or provide feedback on my story I would love to hear from you.

Website	missiondrivenwomensociety.com.au
Email	missiondrivenwomensociety@gmail.com
LinkedIn	linkedin.com/in/michellepavel
Instagram	@money.mindset.meditation
Offer	Become a Society Lady in the Mission Driven Women Society visit missiondrivenwomen.com.au

by Michelle Pavel

Make it **happen!**

The first 40 years of my life, I was a positive, confident, beautiful, happy person who loved to help other people feel good about themselves. People always commented on how inspiring I was, how I had helped them see their situation from a different point of view, how I helped them feel like they could do anything.

I really thought I could do anything and always achieved what I set my mind to. I wasn't aware I was doing anything out of the ordinary, just knew what I wanted and went for it.

I got married to a wonderful man who was romantic, loving, supportive and fun to be around. I gave birth to 3 beautiful souls and my life was rosy.

After 40

When I reached my 40s, and as my children grew, I noticed things starting to change within my marriage. I started to feel controlled, unsupported, manipulated, and very stressed.

by Michelle Pavel

I was experiencing physical pain and my body was seizing up, which I now know was because of the trauma in my life. At the time, however, I didn't realise the cause.

I was the high-income earner, constantly working and exhausted barely getting any breaks. I was looking after everyone, keeping the home functioning, paying the bills, and going through the motions. I felt the weight of the world literally on my shoulders. No wonder I had frozen shoulders! I barely had time for myself and wasn't feeling appreciated for the support I provided my family.

I knew it was time for me to make some changes. Little by little, I started working on healing my body and my mindset.

Mindset shift

A few years later, following a very long drive home from my uninspiring city job, I was tired. I arrived home to an unpleasant environment, and I decided I was done. I was done with my current job, done with my husband, done feeling exhausted, done working my ass off and not having fun with the money I was making.

The next morning, I stood by my bedroom window appreciating the glorious sunshine and clear sky and I asked the Universe for help. I asked it to please send me an opportunity that is perfect for me. I described the exact job specifications, location, hours, salary, and the type of people I wanted to work with, so I could be in a better position to make decisions about my future.

The very next day (yes, the next day!) I received a phone call from an agency contact I hadn't spoken to in years. He had an offer for a role that fitted my exact skillset, income requirements, and all the other wish-list criteria in my request to the Universe. I innately knew the job was for me. I knew there was no better person for the job. I knew this job was going to help set me free.

Within months of working in the new company, it was time for me to be brave. I stopped believing my life was going to get better, regardless of all the attempts to fix things. I didn't believe my kids were happy, so I stood firm, not letting the heart strings hold me back. It was time to give myself and my kids the chance to shine without everyday stress and anxiety.

I dreamt of a calm, relaxing, and peaceful environment so I set out to achieve it.

Moving on, not what I expected

Initially the separation was amicable. After over 20 years of marriage, it was upsetting but still a massive relief. Time at home with the kids was now calm, easy, fun, and relaxing. We had family gatherings and still had fun together, for a while. It wasn't long into the separation I experienced nastiness, accusations, and bitterness from those I chose not to be involved with anymore. This started to destroy my hope and confidence.

People I trusted were no longer trustworthy. I was lonely and I felt totally unsupported and unsure of the future. All the healing work I had done was undone and my stress levels were through the roof. I had to get a grip on the situation or my kids wouldn't have me around for much longer.

I don't like to show my emotions and if you had met me at the time of that trauma, you wouldn't

by Michelle Pavel

have picked it. You would have thought I was strong and capable even though on the inside I was feeling beaten up and dejected.

I went from thinking, "I can do this on my own and I will change the world" to feeling not good enough, not beautiful enough, not young enough... just not enough. I was shattered.

It was tough on the kids, especially my girl. We were separated for a little while. It was excruciating and we both hated it. I didn't fully realise why she chose to live with her father until a year later when I found out his situation wasn't safe. She didn't want him being alone. That is a whole other story and thankfully she has been with me since that situation was exposed.

The boys seemed okay. They felt better off not having to deal with the day-to-day crap but it was still very painful and upsetting for them. They were confused about why my husband and I went from amicable to accusatory and abusive. Me too; so how could I explain it to them?

Healing myself

Years went by. I was still healing and feeling insecure about myself and my contribution to the world. In my job, I was okay. At home, there was always a text message or a statement from someone as a reminder of how I was being treated and how confused and trapped in the middle my kids were. How a loving marriage could turn into such a negative experience was something I wasn't prepared for. I don't know why I was so surprised. I guess I just hoped it would be different. It really sucked the life out of me. All I could do was talk about how I was feeling to a few trusted people, ask the kids to share how they were feeling, and let them know it will be okay. I was trying to stay positive but whenever my confidence started to 'show', someone would bring me down a peg or two.

After COVID hit, I noticed myself becoming a recluse. I wasn't much of a social networker, but I did have some good friends and liked going out occasionally. I wasn't going to the shops or exercising. I was binge watching television and couldn't be bothered with anything much. I added on the kilos, which didn't help my self-esteem. I felt so out of alignment with my own values and I was starting to see that.

Finally, after what felt like forever, I could start to feel myself healing, little by little, chipping away at the limiting beliefs, insecurities, abandonment issues, judgement of myself and others, and trust issues.

My manifesting self was coming back to its glory and my values were starting to realign.

Finding my purpose

I increased my income significantly. I had extra money to spend on nurturing myself for a change, including weekends away and retreats. The pain was starting to leave my body. I had more range of movement and I was starting to believe in myself again. I even had an opportunity to really tell my story to my ex. I think I was heard. That was healing in itself.

My friendships dropped off. Nothing negative, I just decided they weren't aligned with my values. Most of them were going through their own crap and I was past that point now. I needed friends who were positive, successful, confident, and aligned with my new purpose.

What was my purpose exactly? I went on a mission to figure that out.

by Michelle Pavel

Prior to my marriage breakdown several years before, I started on a mission I thought was going to change the world. One business at a time. I started educating local businesses about partnerships and collaborations, sharing ideas for creating win-win opportunities that could change how they bring customers through the door without paying for advertising. That purpose was a very steep uphill climb. Business owners weren't ready for collaborating, their mindset was focused on competition and not complementary partnerships. Those that were ready, didn't take any action. Regardless of the advice or ideas I shared, that fixed mindset was difficult to shift. So eventually I decided I would put my big idea to bed as business owners were not ready to hear it, or maybe I wasn't the right person to be sharing it.

I realised I am a creator. I love coming up with ideas and making things that benefit humanity but to be an influencer was a challenge. Obviously, I still had some limiting beliefs to work through.

My family are happier (removing pandemic from the scenario of course.) Our home is peaceful, calm, relaxing and I feel inspired when I look out at nature in the backyard. We have been in this current home for 5 years... I manifested this as well. When I mentioned before I wanted to feel calm, relaxed, and tranquil, this house fell in my lap. It is private, quiet, lovely, and large enough for us all to have our own space without being on top of each other.

Something was still missing though. I was bored, lonely, and just wanted to have some fun and feel inspired. I wanted to connect with women who also had big ideas like me and who wanted to feel like they could share them without judgement from family and friends who didn't get it.

One summer evening, I was preparing to sleep by saying gratitude statements and winding down with some meditation music. I asked the Universe to help me find some new friends, women who were more aligned with my new spiritual journey. Not woo woos, just more conscious. I also asked for an idea to help me manifest something that could become my new purpose, something I could leave as a legacy for my family and would allow me to help women in local communities find their feet after an upheaval like I had. I was very lucky, I had a great income and despite a lot of things, I felt safe in my environment.

That night, I woke at 2:00 am with an idea to create my own local women's friendship group. I couldn't sleep as I was thinking about it for a little while. This wasn't going to be a normal friendship group, this group was for women on a mission, who had a purpose larger than themselves. I started thinking about who exactly and what exactly did I need in my life right now?

I needed new friendships, yes. But I also needed women in my life who are strong and independent and striving to achieve something amazing with their lives that involves a higher purpose. Ladies who are creative, clever, successful, nurturing, feminine, ambitious, like to have fun, and so on.

I wanted to experience luxury and elegance, returning to my feminine energy that has been dormant for so long, and to help other women increase their net worth through authentic collaborations, and not be bored with a lot of business talk.

I wanted the group to be focused on "it's not just business, it's personal."

I started to consider how other women in my situation may also have the same needs. Maybe they also

by Michelle Pavel

needed to be heard, nurtured, supported, encouraged, empowered, appreciated, recognised, understood, and valued.

I wanted to contribute to helping these women achieve their purpose and remove themselves from situations that aren't in their highest good by empowering them with wisdom, nurturing, support, hope, and guidance from other women collectively.

Wow, from an initial idea to have some more friends, all that came out. I was shocked and excited to get started. I knew it was a long wishlist, but I felt the desire to make it happen and why not?

One of my mottos is... "If you don't ask, you don't get." Thanks, Ghandi.

I consider myself different and I wanted the group to be different. Like nothing seen before. So at 3:00am, I started designing what I could create and how I could bring women together to support each other's growth without feeling competitive, threatened, or judged.

The ideas were flowing. I could create a divine sisterhood. A group for like-minded women who want to make a difference, with us all on our own mission plus a mission to help each other. Where we could experience sharing our message for change in a safe environment, receive guidance from each other, promote our products or services, run events supported by the women in the community, create luxury day retreats, attend society 'networthing' events (yes, I created a new word) to help women grow their networth through partnerships, and most importantly, a community where women can help other women discover, build, and expand their soul tribe.

I think I found it

Since receiving my inspired idea, I have spoken to over 50 purpose-driven women. Each loves the idea of authentically connecting and collaborating with other women who have a like-minded mission to make an impact that will change the world. I also discovered a lot of women in the transition phase of their life looking for their higher purpose. I could tell I was on the right track as women surrounding me were all aligned with what I was working towards.

Fast forward a few months and the group idea has evolved into a Society.

Society means a group who are aligned with the same beliefs, interest or purpose. Plus, I love the image of femininity, elegance, and luxury it evokes. I think we could all do with some of that in our lives.

What now?

This year has been full of manifestations beyond what I ever would have expected a few years ago. Doubling my income within a few months of setting an intention to do so and, little by little, clearing the blocks preventing me from reaching my full potential. There will always be obstacles, but wow... the light at the end of the tunnel is now a glowing expanse highlighting a clearer path.

I feel, together we can grow our communities with our purpose in mind and achieve our goals beyond our wildest dreams.

It is my purpose to help women on a mission dig deep enough to find the hidden treasure within their being so they feel empowered to share their gold and create their own tribe.

Staying on path

It pays to stay hopeful. It was difficult, lonely, disappointing, and frustrating. But you can achieve anything, even when you think it is too late, you are too old, you don't know enough, or you aren't good enough. WE ARE ALL GOOD ENOUGH. We just need to tap into it.

I am grateful for my family and for all the spiritual connections I have made during this time, including amazing people (mostly women) the Universe has brought into my life since I started on my soul mission. They have helped me heal my mind, body, and soul, and given me inspiration.

I would love other women to experience that as well.

It may take me a lot longer to get stuff done these days, but what's the old saying... "Better late than never."

Words of wisdom

If you have a bigger purpose or vision, want to share your voice to create a positive impact, build or expand your own tribe, land your dream job, or create something amazing, then it is up to you to make it happen.

I say to my kids all the time - "Make it Happen!"

I learned from my experience to be stronger, to have courage to speak up, not put up with other people's crap, choose my battles, and go for what I want.

It is up to you to create your legacy and I would love to hear all about your vision.

Dana **Musoiu**

Dana was born and raised in Romania in a town near the capital where everyone knows everyone. When small, she was always attracted to stories. When other children would go and play, she would hang around grownups and listen to their stories and conversations. This planted the seed of determination in her as she noticed the more determined someone was, the more success came their way.

Driven to succeed, Dana studied to be an engineer then, after attending a week of training in Germany, she became determined to live abroad. It took three years, but she finally landed a job in Dubai as a receptionist and moved to the heart of the Middle East, not knowing anyone, just a month after 9/11.

Like many expats in Dubai, Dana flourished as her new international community became a second family. Over the years, she progressed in her career from a receptionist to becoming the passionate Start-Up Coach she is today.

Her secret for success? Caring.

As a Start-Up Coach, Dana inspires and supports her clients to engage in transformational actions to achieve financial freedom. She works with stay-at-home mums-turned-entrepreneurs that are committed to building successful and sustainable businesses. Dana supports her clients by working with them one-on-one and by involving them in the community of mothers she created called Mumpreneurs Dxb. The purpose of the community is to connect, support and inspire each other.

She has chosen to dedicate her time working with these wonderful women as she strongly believes in women helping women and she is a strong advocate of gender equality.

Dana's favourite quote is:

"If you can dream it, you can do it."
Walt Disney

It's by Walt Disney, the world's best dreamer!

Website	danaelenam.com
Email	dana@danaelenam.com
LinkedIn	linkedin.com/in/dana-elena-musoiu-63729713
Facebook	facebook.com/dana.elena.m
Instagram	@dana.elena.m

by Dana Musoiu

The **Hurdler**

Little did I know that a nuclear disaster and a wind from the north had been hacking away at my dream since I was 11 years old…

I've known motherhood was my destiny since I was a young woman leaving Romania at 26-years-old. Nurturing my babies, guiding them through the maze, hugging, holding, feeding and loving them… that was for me. The sleepless nights, worrying about their friendships, their manners and will they fit in? I knew I have to face these things in the future, but that was okay. They would all be worth it because I would have a child to squeeze and love.

Yes, that was my forever map… to be a mum.

Funny how the certainty of youth becomes hazy as the years roll by.

16 years later, I was staring at a list of things I wanted to do in life; things I thought mattered… get married, be a successful coach, earn money, travel, learn new languages, be recognised for my skills and many more.

They were all staring back at me. Working with my coach, Michele, she then told me to strike out all the things that didn't matter. I was left with two... *Mother and Grandmother*. Michele had helped me connect with the deep inner longings time and circumstances had made me avoid. How could I have been so silly for so long?

The answer came to me in a flash. A toxic relationship I had just escaped after arriving in Dubai had left me scarred so deeply that it took me ten years to get myself together. That's why I had buried the importance of *mother* and *grandmother*. It was to protect myself as my reality at the time meant these were not even the remotest of possibilities. You see, it was ten years of failed attempts to make men date me for more than a month. Ten years of feeling like a failure every time someone around me got married. Ten years of jealousy every time they had children. Ten years of watching this through the eyes of a single woman wondering when her turn at happiness would sweep her off her feet.

To make myself feel better, I lied. I said I was fine. I said it was too late anyway to have children. I told myself that not everyone has children and that I have other things to make me happy like finally being with this wonderful man, Ben, whom I'd been dating for over three years, our 2 cats and of course helping people in my work as a coach. That should be enough, right? Anyway, we were too old to have children.

Yet there I was, staring at *mother* and *grandmother* while all the other things on the list seemed to mock me.

So what now?

When younger, I would choose the easy way out every single time. I did that both times I was pregnant in my early twenties. I know what you're thinking... "How could she?" But no, it wasn't the right time I told myself, not knowing how much I would regret it later. Somehow this time, the easy way didn't seem so easy...

Talking about my list with Ben was tricky. How do you come back to someone and tell them you have changed your mind about such a huge subject? He was very confused when I raised the topic. Apart from telling him how much I wanted a baby, I also asked him to imagine how would it feel waking up in the morning and seeing a baby's face smiling at you; you being their whole world. All those thoughts from when I left Romania came flooding back because that image for me was still pure bliss. Yet, it wasn't easy for Ben to share my dream of 20 years. We talked about it on and off because I was now unable to let it go. Life isn't about the easy path, it's about the fulfilling path.

I knew I was one step closer when he asked me, "Can we still have babies though?" I never doubted that. We were both healthy, non-smokers and only socially drinking.

Yet little did I know that a nuclear disaster and a wind from the north had been hacking away at my dream since I was 11 years old...

After about 6 months of conversations, we decided to give it a try. When a few attempts to have babies in the traditional way failed, we went to an IVF clinic to test ourselves. Ben's results were perfect. Mine not so. I had a 0.15% chance of becoming pregnant. Who do I have to thank for that? "Chernobyl," the doctor said. "There are many women like you."

So what now?

by Dana Musoiu

Do I just stop and forget about this new hurdle or continue and see what comes up? I knew deep down that I would regret it later if I didn't try everything. My heart was sinking, I felt like I was holding onto the last straw. And I continued digging up hope by trusting technology in these amazing times when everything seems possible.

I started the first round of IVF, pills and injections in my thighs until they become blue. Two weeks later in the clinic, I found out my eggs were so tiny and that it was impossible to create a healthy embryo. I thought, well, this is it... it didn't work. I was a few years too late. "*Get yourself together and be happy with what you have, Dana!*"

Deep inside I hurt and hurt and hurt. I regretted all the wasted time. More than that, I regretted how I lost the 2 chances given to me to be a mum. I wished badly that I could turn back time. I was busy feeling sorry for myself when the doctor started saying there is another option.

Donor eggs.

You mean the baby won't be genetically mine? Another hurdle. And this one required a second opinion...

To Ben's surprise, I travelled back home to Romania to a well-respected clinic for this second opinion on my fertility. It was a rainy spring day when I drove with my dad to the clinic feeling hopeful. The doctor looked at the test results and gave me the same diagnosis. My eggs were too small.

I remember getting back into my dad's car and breaking into tears. Dad said, "A child is a child and even with a donor's egg, she will still be your baby and you will love her the same."

So, now I feel I need to explain something and you might not like me for it...

For a few years to that point, every time I heard someone adopted a baby, I wondered, how does it feel when the mother looks at her child and doesn't recognise herself. I assumed it was hard. I was turning the question around now. How would I feel when I look at my child and I don't see myself? I was afraid I would not love him the same. I was struggling with this. Dad's words made me see how it really was. I loved every baby I ever met. I knew I had the capacity to love and that helped me decide to use a donor's egg.

A month later from Dubai, I was in contact with a clinic in Prague. Why Prague? Because not many countries offered the donor egg procedure and Ben thought it would be a great place to visit! I started taking the medicine and the shots again, this time in my stomach... they leave fewer bruises there!

We visited the clinic and Ben's sperm was matched with the donor's egg. We waited for few days to have the embryo ready before it was implanted in me. The first time I saw the small embryo, which needed to be magnified on the screen, filled me with tears. The whole pain I had been through didn't matter anymore. I was pregnant and this time nothing was going to stop me having this baby.

I came back to Dubai determined to wait for a week to do the test. The doctor had said to do it only after a week, not earlier than that. This is because it might be a false negative which will stress me emotionally and could make me lose the baby.

But of course...

I didn't wait.

I tested before that and, yes... it was negative. We were both devastated. All the happiness and joy of less than a week ago had disappeared and were replaced with self-doubt, anxiety and, yes, a little bit of, "How could I have believed it would be that easy?"

So the next hurdle had appeared. Give up or continue?

As I recovered, I told myself I would try three times in total as I'd heard stories of women who have done it for years and it affected their health and their relationships. Besides, the age cap to do this procedure was 44. I didn't have many years left.

The clinic asked me if I want to start again in the following month or wait for a few months. I was determined to succeed. I went straight back to pills and injections and three weeks later was back in Prague for another round. This time I was by myself as Ben had to work.

When I met the doctor, I told him that I wanted 2 embryos implanted this time. He warned me about the risks of having twins at my age. After failing the first time with only one embryo, I thought it was a good idea to double up the bets. I was staying at a friend's house during this time and I only told her I was doing IVF, nothing about donor's egg. I didn't feel comfortable telling her that. She asked a few times about the egg extraction process and I was vague about it. She dropped it after a while. I am not sure why I didn't want to say. Maybe it was because I felt I was failing in some way because of being incapable of having my own child. It wasn't only her I didn't tell. No one knew what I was doing apart from my parents and Ben.

Certain inadequacies I didn't want public.

Again I found myself looking at the screen with my name on it and once again I saw the small embryo. This time I said, "Hi, it is nice to meet you, my baby."

Soon, another issue began to bubble to the surface...

When we started the procedures in Prague, we also started talking about getting married. You see, if I became pregnant, we would need to get married as these were the rules in Dubai. (A hurdle? Yes, but a much smaller one.) Ben had told me before how weddings made him feel, how being in the centre of attention felt like a dread. This time he said he would marry me if there was no big ceremony and not many people around. For me, it was exactly the opposite. I wanted to be the centre of attention and have family and friends around. I wanted to be princess for a day. One of the things I learned in coaching was about showing empathy by meeting the people where they are. I loved Ben with all my heart and we were about to have a baby together and if a small ceremony is what it takes for us to get married, so be it.

After a little Googling, we found Denmark to be a country that enables speedy marriages. We contacted a wedding planner and decided to get married just after the second round of IVF. I arrived from Prague on a Thursday and two days later we took the plane to Copenhagen. We kept it secret from everyone until the last moment. We called our parents one day before to tell them. My mum was very happy to hear the news, my dad and brother... not so much happy. In fact, they were very disappointed they were not there. Same for Ben's parents.

I remember the church outside Copenhagen. I remember walking down the aisle alone in my wedding dress. I remember Ben waiting for me. That was the moment when I wished my family was there.

by Dana Musoiu

This was not how I imagined my marriage would begin and, in the moment, it made me sad. It was the two of us and two friends from Copenhagen as witnesses. My mum told me my brother cried when he saw me alone. Ben's sister too. After the ceremony we had lunch at a restaurant near the church. I threw the bouquet to a waiter. We headed back to Copenhagen. We were married. Done and simple.

When we arrived back in Copenhagen, Ben felt hungry. McDonald's served us hamburgers for our first dinner as man and wife.

We chose to get married one day before Ben's birthday to make sure we celebrate them separately in the future. This meant we had three major days aligned... wedding day, Ben's birthday and my pregnancy test day.

This time, I had decided to wait to do the test! With everything what was happening, I didn't have time to think about it until the morning of the test. We were in a Radisson Blue Hotel in Sweden. I peed on a stick and a plus sign appeared. What does this mean? I bought the test from Prague and everything was in Czech! Ben used a translator app. It was positive! I started jumping up and down. I couldn't believe it. I was pregnant. I am going to be a mother. Could it be possible? The whole day my face was beaming with joy. I felt my body already changing, my breasts were swollen and tender. Two days later, we arrived in Dubai and that feeling was gone. I was convinced it was a false positive and spent the whole day in bed feeling miserable. I made an appointment with the doctor but a sense of foreboding had overcome me... I was definitely not pregnant. That's too good to be true. I was dreading the next round of injections, traveling to Prague on my own, the painful procedure and getting my hopes high only to be disappointed again. I could see it all happening. I went to the doctor feeling hopeless. The email came with the result. It couldn't have been good news, I was sure of that. I called Ben to open it together... I wasn't brave enough to do it alone. And there it was... the test was positive and we were going to be parents. I couldn't believe my luck. I now knew, I was going to be a mother. And not just any mother... a Goddamn excellent one!

And this is how my pregnancy began. I had to take pills and inject myself in the stomach for the next three months to make sure that the pregnancy took and I didn't care anymore. Ben waited for three months to share the news. There is a tradition for westerners to wait for the first trimester. We don't do such things in Romania. I told my parents right away.

After 9 months we had a baby boy, healthy and perfect in every way. I couldn't sleep for the first 24 hours of his life. My senses were wide awake. I was thrilled with excitement. I breastfed him for a year and added 16 kgs in the process. Our son is 2 years and 5 months as I type this chapter, he goes to nursery and is learning his ways. I want my son to know that I'm his biological mother and he has a genetic mother somewhere in Czech Republic. I'm still trying to find the right way and right time to tell him. Not many people know, including Ben's family, that Joe was conceived the way he was. I will share it one day. Writing here is the first step to getting it out there. Telling the truth right now is lifting a weight off me.

Ben and I have thought about it many times... what would people think when they see us with our son? We know they will wonder if we are his parents or grandparents, like I did many times before with other people. I also know that one day Joe will ask me why

I am not as young as his friends' mothers. He might even be subject to bullying at school because of it. And, like many other things in life, I will deal with it as it happens. I wish Ben and I were younger for Joe's benefit and at the same time I'm grateful that he came at a time when I was ready to be his mum.

I'm forever grateful to Michele, the coach who uncovered the need in me to be a mother. And to Ben for embarking on this journey with me and to the anonymous woman who gave me a part of her. She made it possible for me to be a mother to this amazing, beautiful child of mine. I look into his eyes every day and no, I don't recognise myself in his physical features, he looks mostly like his dad. Yet now I know the answer to my question of before... How would I feel when I look at him and don't see myself? I feel infinite love for him, just like my dad said I would. I do I recognise myself in him... he is kind and full of life. We share that. I'm so glad I overcame all those trying hurdles so I now have the honour of being his mother.

After all, it's all I ever wanted to be.

Liz **Grant**

In many ways I've led a charmed life. I had an uncomplicated childhood in regional Australia, I went to university when it was still free (just). And I've worked in all aspects of building, growing and managing a business and now have my own business helping others build, grow and manage theirs. But as someone who always expected themselves to do and be the best – and often not quite getting there – I've also had my share of self-generated disappointment.

Over the years I've learned a number of ways to pick myself up and get going again when I lose my way – either because I've failed spectacularly, or because I'm doing things that don't inspire me - and I enjoy passing these tools onto others. And for me, key to all of this is knowing your 'why'; having that north star that sets boundaries, provides focus and gives you a reason to purposefully connect with others.

But knowing your 'why' and living your 'why' are different. I've learned that to live purposefully, you need to look after yourself and have a support team that has your back. We're all on our own journey and how we structure that journey and feel at any time is ours to own. And that's something I'm passionate about doing and helping others find and create for themselves.

Website	yourcustomers.com.au
Email	liz@yourcustomers.com.au
LinkedIn	linkedin.com/in/lizgrant
Facebook	facebook.com/whatyourcustomerswant
Instagram	instagram.com/what_your_customers_want
Twitter - Business	twitter.com/WhatCustmrsWant
Twitter - Personal	twitter.com/LizMGrant

From burnout to balance:
A journey by design

I don't know what triggered my crying. But there I was, on a Zoom with colleagues, bursting into tears, sobbing. I was at breaking point and knew I had to do something because this wasn't the first time I'd been here...

It had been 13 years since I remembered waking up at three in the morning with my heart pounding, my left arm in pain, not able to move and thinking, Is this it? Am I having a heart attack? After about an hour, the pain subsided and I was able to breathe normally again. It was only after the fifth time in as many weeks that I had woken like this that I resolved to do something.

This time, I wasn't going to sit and wait to see if things just got better on their own.

13 years ago, the cause of my panic attacks was obvious. I was at the peak of what had been a fast-paced and successful career. I was responsible for a large team and significant profit and to get anything done required working with multiple stakeholders who had their own

agendas. But I also enjoyed what I was doing. My team made a positive impact on the company's customers and everyday had a new challenge.

This time, it was harder to figure out what was causing my breakdown. We were financially stable as a family and extended family during a pandemic when many of my friends and colleagues were not so lucky. I felt like I had no right to feel depleted given my circumstances. But I was. I just felt sad and lethargic and couldn't figure out why.

My work had fundamentally changed from helping small businesses access support and growth opportunities from the grass roots to administering support programs. I was seeing what else these businesses needed, but I didn't have the access, resources or permission to make it happen.

I started journaling again. Instead of having conversations in my head about the way of the world, I wrote everything down. These weren't organised thoughts, nor were they the ramblings of a mad woman. They were just a way I could develop different positions and work through what was on my mind. Once the stories were on paper staring up at me, I could gain perspective and shift into a more positive mindset.

I came to realise I had lost the key element I had painstakingly developed over the past 13 years – a sense of purpose. So even though my financial security need was being met, I still felt disempowered as I was unable to actually help people. I was doing the do, but it felt meaningless.

At the same time, I was still trying to be superwoman. I was working full-time, home schooling, managing the house and trying to be there for family and friends. But I wasn't tending to my needs. It wasn't the volume of things I was doing; my cup was simply empty. I had nothing left. Absolutely nothing. I needed to start doing more of the things that gave me energy and less of the things that depleted that energy. After all, I needed to be there for my family at the end of the day.

Filling the 'cup'

The first thing I did was resolve to start filling that cup again. It was going to be difficult to pick myself up while I was exhausted. I resolved to get some sleep and change perspective on the things I couldn't change so they no longer drained me. I needed to do the things I knew would restore my energy.

I started to be more purposeful about what I ate. I reduced sugar, simple carbohydrates and alcohol and ate more vegetables and hearty soups. I took up swimming. It was something I could do at the beginning of the day when the rest of the house was still asleep. This way my swim didn't get waylaid once the workday started. And I slept... if I needed a ten-minute powernap during the day, I took it, and I didn't feel guilty.

I also reconnected with friends and colleagues in a way that was purposeful. I asked them how they were going and offered to help because that's what I loved to do. I started saying "no" to things, particularly anything I knew I would struggle to do because of the energy it would take.

Then I set about to rediscover my why. According to Dan Beuttner, author of The Blue Zones, maintaining a strong sense of inner purpose is one of the common characteristics of people who live the longest. I re-read Find Your Why. In it, Simon Sinek talks about how we are fundamentally connected to purpose. Further, states Sinek, to find this purpose, we need to look back on what has driven us in the past. Accordingly, I wrote down those moments I could remember when I was in flow state, where I was so happy that I didn't notice time passing.

I had often said that what was important to me was having no boundaries – not putting boundaries on myself, my friends nor my family. With this mindset, anything is possible with the right tools, knowledge and support. I also realised that I aimed to always leave a situation better than it was when I arrived. This extends to everything I do. I love helping people discover what they love doing and adding to their tools, knowledge, support and mindset so they can create a life doing whatever that is.

In each of these moments I'm facilitating growth through adding value. I was clear, I knew I needed to get back to adding value – growing in myself, my circumstances and helping others go beyond what they thought was possible.

I discovered finding great role models can make a difference. I needed people whose behaviour I admired so I could see what I needed to do to achieve the results they achieved. When I thought about living my purpose and knowing how to prioritise, my mum has always been a great role model...

My mum worked to create a better life for children with an intellectual disability. In addition to her teaching role, she taught music, organised excursions and tried to find as many ways as she could to give them joy. And she still managed to replenish herself. Mum loved to travel. That was her thing. When dad didn't want to travel to the overseas locations on her list, she would find girlfriends to travel with and come back with stories and gifts and pen pals – people she still writes to today. I've always admired this about her. She was always there for us because she kept her cup filled.

At the time, it wasn't enough for me to merely get more sleep, know my why and have role models. I also needed to become who I needed to be. When I'm preparing to speak to large audiences, I always ask myself, who do I need to be today? What is it I want this audience to take away and who do I need to be to ensure that happens? Sometimes that's an authority. Sometimes that's someone nurturing. Sometimes that's someone inspiring or energising. Then I get into the mindset of the person who can create that for the audience. This time, I was creating the mindset for the person living my why.

Sharing the load

Motivational speaker Jim Rohn said you are the average of the five people you spend the most time with. Recent research shows you're not only influenced by those in your immediate circle, but by their circles as well.

After working with hundreds of business owners, Jen Harwood in her book, The Greatness Principle, proposes there are eight roles we need in our lives to help us become and stay great. These are —

- The Sage, who knows you at your core and calls you out when you're not being true to yourself
- The Scholar, who helps you build on your ideas and make them even greater
- The Grounder, whose job is to be the realist or the cynic, and can help you see the risks in what you do
- The Anchor who has an unshakeable belief in you and helps you see possibility
- The Catalyst, who causes you to step up
- The Motivator who holds you to account

- The Enthusiast, who thinks everything you do is amazing
- The Bystander whom you can download to and, because they're not invested in what you're doing, can listen without judgement or even comment.

In looking at these eight roles, I had to make some hard decisions. It's unfair to expect any individual to take on more than one role. So, I thought about who was fulfilling these roles for me. Was I expecting anyone to take on more than one role? And where were the gaps? I started to seek out people I knew had my back and rebuild my circle.

Sometimes you don't know who people are for you until you have a conversation. So, I started to share where I was at and where I was planning to go to see where they would take it. Would they point out the risks, build on my ideas, cheer me on, or just listen with no attachment like I was downloading? After a couple of months, I was able to connect with my friends and colleagues more purposefully and it was clear they were also being energised from our conversations. I now have people in my circle that I can connect with to hold me accountable, to help take my ideas further and to point out what can go wrong so I can think about this before I leap.

I also started to think about who I was for other people. I'm usually the motivator or catalyst, but many of my colleagues weren't in a mindset to have me take on these roles for them at the time. So, I became an enthusiast and bystander while making sure I wasn't taking on more than one role for any one person.

In doing this, I could feel my energy building – not just because I was getting something back from people, but also because I could give purposefully to my friends and colleagues again.

In reconnecting more purposefully, I was also able to listen more readily and objectively and be who my friends and colleagues needed me to be in the moment. As others strengthened and gained more energy, they were able to support me as well.

Sharing my 'why'

At the beginning of every year, I create a new vision board. I start my vision, not with goals, but with actually visualising where I want to be at the end of the next three to five years; what's the next phase, what is the impact I want to have, the legacy I want to leave and what does that look like for how I should be living life now?

When the vision is clear, I think about what it might look like at the end of the year, the end of six months, one month, next week. The goals become part of how I get there rather than the destination. Even once I've set goals, I don't lose sight of the original vision. Sometimes the how has to change; there are always many ways to achieve a vision.

Many people don't feel vision boards and having a purpose are necessary. For me, they set boundaries and help me focus on what is important in my life. So, my vision board included getting back into my business full-time, having more time with my family and making time every day to do things that filled my cup.

Having done the work to get out of superwoman funk, I was determined not fall back into it. This meant not only prioritising what I was doing, but also enlisting the help of others to help me get stuff done. So, I've been nurturing relationships with friends and asking for help when needed. And I'm ready for them to say "no" as I recognise they also have busy lives.

What's happened since I've been reconnecting, rebuilding relationships and sharing ideas is that more opportunities have come up both to collaborate and also to grow personally. I've had introductions to great people and work – work that actually inspires me!

Sometimes people say, "Don't share your dream, because someone else might steal it." But the thing is, it's your dream, not someone else's. As long as you keep putting one foot in front of the other and go for your dream, no one can steal it from you. It's yours to make happen.

I shared my vision with my family and they added to it. We discussed what was important to us all and, as a result, we decided to move back to a farm but this time near the beach. Where we're moving to is two and half hours away from where we are, so it's a new community and a new business community. But, once again, as soon as I started putting it out there and sharing my vision for what I wanted to create, people came forward with introductions, ideas and opportunities. I now have many referrals and I'm already starting to build a network.

People ask me if I'm nervous about moving and I say, "No, I'm excited!" because I know I've done the work and I know I'm where I'm meant to be. It doesn't stop there, of course. Everyday I work on replenishing my energy by getting enough sleep, journaling and getting out into nature. I keep connecting with friends, colleagues and family and checking in with my why. I know my priorities, my family is excited and I've got the right people in my circle. In fact, if anything, there's a sense of peace and excitement at the same time. And that's a great place to be.

Justine **Martin**

This definition has been the cornerstone of Justine Martin's extraordinary journey over the last decade, a journey no one could fathom, but in her words ... this journey has changed Justine for the better.

Ten years ago she was diagnosed with Multiple Sclerosis, then three primary cancers and also underwent three heart surgeries. Justine was told she would never work again. But that was never an option for her!

Justine catapulted herself into the world of business. She not only changed her life to give it purpose & direction, but also inspired those around her with her story.

After learning how to paint and using her art as therapy, she has become a multi-award-winning artist and found the strength and determination to take control of her financial future. Her own journey inspired the passion and launch of Resilience Mindset; a second business where she coaches, launched a podcast series, is writing a number of books and does public speaking on resilience – a topic so close to her heart, to help others.

Justine was humbled to be recognised for her achievements and outstanding contributions for people living with disabilities in Greater Geelong; awarded the '2021 Geelong Awards for People with Disability'.

Justine now runs four businesses, is a National Ambassador/Public Speaker for MS Australia and won SEVEN national business awards in 2021 including GOLD at the AusMumpreneur Awards for 'Coach of the Year' and GOLD in the Roar Awards for Creative 'Artist of the Year'.

Email	hello@justinemartin.com.au
LinkedIn	linkedin.com/company/justine-martin-corporation
Linktree	linktr.ee/justinemartincorporation
Website. Bus.	justinemartin.com.au
Facebook. Bus.	facebook.com/resiliencemindsetwithjustinemartin
Instagram. Bus.	@resiliencemindsetjustinemartin
Website. Art	juztart.com.au
Facebook. Art	facebook.com/justinemartinartist
Instagram. Art	@juzt_art

by Justine Martin

In the blink of an eye

Time is the most precious commodity on the planet. You can't buy it, sell it, reuse it or even borrow it. Be careful how you spend it and who you spend it on. This has become the driving force in my life, particularly during the last 10 years...

With trembling hands, a booming heart and an anxious expression, I sat across from him knowing what he was about to say. His authoritative lips were moving, mouthing words no one should ever hear. As my world spun a dizzy web of how, if, when and why, one clear thought entered the confusion, "How could this be happening to me?" But then, what made me think I was so special that it couldn't happen to me? Like many my age, I had been naïve, blasé and self-absorbed in my own little world. In fact, the list could go on. Yet there I was, sitting opposite the doctor and listening to him say I had the same incurable disease which substantially contributed to my mother's premature death.

by Justine Martin

In the blink of an eye, that carefree, naïve, time abusive, girl was forever gone. I stood in front of the mirror and stared into my eyes. Numbness, anger and fear consumed me. Yet to the outside world I suddenly didn't feel part of, my appearance was the same. A diagnosis of Multiple Sclerosis can do that to you. My brother and myself had grown up our whole lives being told we couldn't get MS, yet here I was with it! How was I going to tell my children and extended family? Was I going to die too soon like mum at 49? As the world spun faster and faster, I felt more and more nauseous and just wanted it to stop!

Then came those heartbreaking phone calls. One by one; my grandparents, brother, aunty and uncle and son, who all lived over 3000km away on the east coast of Australia, received the news. Then my fiancé who was away working in the mines. Yes, I was all alone, scared and anxious and simply needed a hug. But I had to stay strong in front of my daughter. That first night home alone in Perth, I curled up into a little ball and cried myself to sleep terrified of what my life was about to become.

For the next month, I stayed working in the dream job I had spent my whole career working towards. It helped fill my days, occupied my mind, killed time. There were lots of tears. So, so many tears. Without doubt, I was slowly losing control. And physically, there were so many simple day-to-day tasks I could no longer perform as the lesions throughout the branches of my central nervous system were preventing the messages from getting through. The evidence was clear... my body was failing me.

I started to see a counsellor to try to stop the world from spinning out of control. It helped but I still felt so alone. I had to stop work due to my symptoms.

Unfortunately, I couldn't count very well, that part of my brain was gone, permanently damaged. The technical term is cognitive impairment. I had trouble staying awake, fatigue was debilitating. I was beyond tired, something I'd never experienced before even in my younger partying days. This was very different. I had zero energy. Just forming sentences was a struggle. I would fall asleep mid-sentence.

Going on extended sick leave was my only option. My employer told me that the big bosses wouldn't like me taking three months off and that I was to quit my job!!! What? I loved my work helping other people.

I'm not a quitter. Never was, never will be. Failure is never an option, yet here was someone telling me to quit! What would my purpose be if I couldn't work? How was I going to cope without going to work every day? The simple answer is, I didn't. I plummeted into a dark downward spiral ending in a big black hole. Sleeping became my life for nearly three months, even sleeping through doctor's appointments and school pick-ups.

I went from a well-paid job and financial independence to nothing in the blink of an eye and became solely reliant on someone else to feed us, put a roof over my and my children's heads. Not something I ever thought could happen at the age of 40, and definitely not something one plans for.

I had hit rock bottom. I was losing my independence at a rapid rate. What remained of life looked bleak.

I was terrified.

I questioned what would be my purpose if I could no long contribute financially to my family. I had been brought up with a huge work ethic. What use would I ever be to anyone if I could no longer work, let alone contributing to society in paying my taxes? Depression was starting to set in.

It was humiliating. I was so embarrassed and felt like there wasn't a damn thing I could do about it.

My neurologist suggested finding a hobby as I was going to have a lot of time on my hands. I had always wanted to learn how to paint but had never made the time. It always seemed that focussing on my career and family was more important. Now, all I had was time coupled with a growing anxiety that made everything ten times worse.

I decided to join an art class at a studio a friend owned. I drove to that class every week for three months yet never mustered the courage to get out of the car. I would sit there, wanting to go inside, willing myself to go inside but the crippling fear got the better of me. I would drive home crying. I was so ashamed of the person I was becoming. So home I went... to the same four walls that seemed to be mocking me and suffocating what little life I had left. Home had become a jail and MS was the warden.

One day, when sitting in my car something just snapped in me. I got angry at myself. I got out of my car and walked through the damn doors. This courage was born out of frustration and a yearning to get off this hamster wheel. I thought, what's the worst that could happen?

Inside, I found a whole new world and a form of expression I was not only capable of, but... I was good at it! Creating seemed to take me into a form of meditation. The more I created, the more I felt calm and in control. Slowly, through painting, I started to live again and my self-worth began adding up to so much more than the sum of my disabilities.

A move from Perth to Geelong, to be surrounded by family for support, saw some major changes in me. I entered my first art exhibition with able-bodied artists. To my amazement, I sold my first piece for $300! It took 12 months from the time my world crashed, but I had earned my own money! I can't stress this enough.... this was my money! Money, I had earned. It was monumental. I realised I could still contribute to society and support my family. I didn't feel like such a burden. I had a purpose again and wasn't just a waste of space.

I was becoming pliable and adapting to the circumstances around me. Silly as it sounds, my pieces of art were teaching me resilience without me even knowing it was happening.

My little art hobby started to grow. I won a scholarship through MS Australia to buy art supplies. This allowed me to spend hours creating pieces and traveling to my happy place. Like many happy places, mine was an incubator for ideas...

My mind started racing. What could I really achieve with my artwork? Drawing on my retail and marketing background from various multi-level marketing businesses (MLMs) and owning a fashion boutique, I knew setting up a small business around my art was possible. After all, the basics were in place – saleable products and a marketplace willing to purchase. Importantly, starting from scratch meant the business could be structured around my needs and it could grow into bigger and better things.

Empowerment started coursing through my veins. Suddenly, choices were available, decisions needed to be made and planning for the future was occurring. Being disabled was no longer the perennial thought debilitating my being. Instead,

by Justine Martin

my mind was swimming with ifs, what ifs, why nots and how hard can that be?

I could finally dream again.

Juzt art was born.

I entered every exhibition I could find. To my surprise, awards started flowing, more than 40 so far! And, it still floors me... People Buy My Art! You have no idea how incredibly important that is to me. I can contribute! An opportunity to take over the wall space in Café Zoo in Drysdale came my way. I took it with both hands and filled those walls with my creations. In doing so, Juzt art Gallery started creating a buzz.

I went through all the stages of grief – shock and denial, pain and guilt, anger and bargaining, depression, reconstruction and finally, acceptance and hope. This process didn't happen overnight. It took three years. Not every day is a good day, but the good days outweigh the bad.

People often ask what drives me to succeed? One thing is having the power of choice. There are so many things I choose to do. I have been as low as a person can be, homeless with two young children and having to live on handouts from charities. The one thing I learned from that humbling experience is that you have the choice to remain in that mindset or choose a better way of life. We all have the power of change within us. These days, mind maps are an effective tool I recommend when looking for change. You never know what's going to come out.

Learning to live with a disease like MS takes time. If you listen, your body will teach you what, when, how and if certain actions can or cannot be undertaken. You can fight your personal City Hall or go with the edicts she issues. There's no right or wrong answer.

But here's what you can't do with MS or any other disease, you can't use it to tell you what else is going on in your body. Just because you may feel you're coming to terms with one thing, doesn't mean other nefarious cells aren't devising their own plot...

Within a 6-month period in 2016, I was diagnosed with melanoma, stage IV Lymphoma and Leukemia. Yep, three primary cancers all at once. Additionally, there was a clotting problem called Livedo Reticularis and too much protein in my blood causing Mixed Cryoglobulinemia which was choking all my internal organs. There's no other way to say this, I was dying.

One of the hardest things was having to tell my children what I was facing. I'm greedy, I wanted to live. Dying wasn't going to be the choice for me. Through this time, I remained as positive as I could. I devised a daily routine beginning with getting out of bed every single day then making it. Regardless of what the rest of the day held, at least I had accomplished something. Besides, nothing is nicer than sliding into a made bed.

I lost the ability to hold a pen and paint brush while going through chemotherapy. So I continued on just using my fingers. Creating art had become a lifeline and form of meditation for me and I was not willing to let go it. It was also part of my self-care.

The cancers are in full remission and I am able to once again use a paintbrush these days. Though I still often use the element of finger painting in my creations and now even teach Finger-Painting for Grown Ups. I guess every cloud has a silver lining if you look for it. In fact, this lining just keeps getting shinier as recently I began collaborating with another author in this book, Liz Grant. Together, we are "Team

Fingerprint." We work in the corporate sector helping with team building through discovering their team vision and purpose before creating a team painting encapsulating these.

Throughout my cancer journey, I realised I owned a job not a business. If I didn't work, I didn't get paid. Unlike most, MS doesn't allow me to rely on my body. So how was I going to continue to make an income while being unable to work? The simple answer was to create residual income to take the pressure off. Becoming an author, designing online resilience courses and starting a publishing house have all added to my residual income.

Throughout my troubles, my passion for helping others has not waned. This drive has led me to increasing my purpose to assist people who are struggling to bounce back after adversity. My company, Resilience Mindset, is all about this and through it I'm able to pass on my strategies to others while reminding myself of the power we all have to go out and grab our better futures.

I have faced many more adversities in the last 10 years – heart surgeries, broken bones, relationship breakups and deaths. Each adversity has built more resilience to help overcome the next. I still see a counsellor regularly to off load everything as it's not my family or friend's responsibility to carry this burden.

10 years have passed since I first picked up that paint brush and changed my world. That passion gave me back my control and a future I never thought possible when I was staring at four walls and heading down that dark hole. That paint brush led me to becoming an award-winning artist, winning gold '2021 Creative

Artist of the Year' through Roar Success. From there I won gold for 'Coach of the Year' and silver and bronze awards through AusMumpreneur. Now, I'm proud to have taken the next step of helping others like myself by teaching disabled people Juzt art Wellness Classes.

I am known as the 'Queen of Resilience' because of all the adversities I have faced. Some people call me Wonder Woman. I am just me... a woman who knows what she wants and how much work it's going to take to achieve those goals despite facing daily struggles.

I don't live in the past. Instead, I live every day to the fullest and my big dreams and even bigger goals keep me on course. You only die once, so live every single day to the maximum. Courage doesn't mean you don't get afraid. Courage means you don't let fear stop you. People call me inspirational. I'd much rather be known as motivational as I actively help others achieve their goals.

Never ever give up on your own dreams. You don't know how far they will take you!

"It's comforting being part of a tight community where we all have each other's backs because, every now and then, we are called on to prioritise this love for our hometown and put others' needs ahead of our own..."
Elizabeth Keeley

Elizabeth **Keeley**

I have been a small business owner for 15 years, running my own Mobile Dog Wash Business in Townsville, North Queensland.

While I still own my business in Townsville, I recently moved to Brisbane to take up an opportunity at our Company's Head Office as the Franchise Business Manager for Aussie Pooch Mobile.

My 'North Star' is my driving passion for helping others succeed in business, to be a mentor and a support for other like-minded Business owners. Caring for Dogs has always been at the core of who I am and where my passion started, this shows in the business I have built and the other like-minded Individuals and community groups I surround myself with.

My Top 3 accomplishments in business are being able to provide the opportunity for others to do what I do, to be recognised within Aussie Pooch Mobile and win multiple awards at our annual awards, and last year to be recognised and win a National Franchising award from the Franchise Council of Australia.

Outside of work I am a wife and a mother. I love the beach and the Ocean, but also enjoy the thrill of running along trails through the bush. When I relax it is usually sitting and reading a good book, or watching a movie with my daughter and my dogs at my side.

Have a Pawsome day!

Email	apmlizkeeley@gmail.com
LinkedIn	linkedin.com/in/elizabeth-keeley-23a56b202
Instagram	instagram.com/@lizzyklyfe
Website, Bus.	AussiePoochMobile.com.au
Facebook, Bus.	facebook.com/AussiePoochMobile
Instagram, Bus.	@aussiepoochofficial
Shop, Bus.	shop.aussiepm.com.au
Article, Case Study	whichfranchise.net.au/index.cfm?event=getCaseStudy&articleId=652

It never rains.
It pours.

Townsville is a cruisy place to live. Situated on the north coast of Queensland, it's sun-drenched and warm most of the year. We attract many students who study at James Cook University and loads of tourists who are looking for that idyllic tropical getaway.

As we're small, there are only a few degrees of separation between the locals and, consequently, we tend to look after each other. It's comforting being part of a tight community where we all have each other's backs because, every now and then, we are called on to prioritise this love for our hometown and put others' needs ahead of our own...

Wednesday 30th January 2019.

It's been raining heavily for the last 6 days due to a slow-moving tropical low situated east of Mt Isa. For the meteorology buffs out there, it's embedded in a stalled, but a vigorously active, monsoon trough. It's brought the Ross River Dam, situated upstream of Townsville, to 112% capacity. That's nothing new for us. We either suffer monsoon floods in January/February or extreme drought.

I own and run a mobile dog wash business in Townsville, Aussie Pooch Mobile. I have 5 others who work with me in the business running trailers and we all love what we do. During the last 12 years, we have built a wonderful little business that is fun, busy, and very rewarding. Oh... and the dogs love it too!

In the afternoon, my husband called me. "You better come home. There's a lot more rain coming, and they are advising everyone to get off the roads unless necessary." I am no stranger to working in the rain, so I wasn't fazed. However, as most of my jobs had cancelled due to the weather, a hot cup of tea and some dry clothes sounded like heaven.

It can be hard running a small business when your only source of income dries up in wet weather. Nonetheless, we've been through it before and know as soon as the rain clears, we'll be flooded with calls so wet, smelly, muddy dogs can be made huggable again. We know we just need to ride out the storm.

But this storm wasn't going anywhere in a hurry...

Thursday 31st January.

To describe this tropical low as persistent would be a gross understatement. It was tenacious. Having sucked up billions of litres of water from the Gulf of Carpentaria, it was now determined to furiously dump them all in the catchment of the Ross River. All this water was now quickly making its way into the Ross River Dam, only 20km from the centre of Townsville.

As a community, we were more than nervous.

We were scared.

When a large dam upstream of your town is holding more than 100% of its capacity and there is no sign of the rain letting up, decisions need to be made that will affect the health and livelihoods of people downstream.

The first decision was to open an Evacuation Centre for those initially impacted by the rising river levels. Then, at 1.36pm, the Ross River Dam gates open automatically in line with the Emergency Action Plan (EAP) as the water level exceeded 100%.

But there was still a fundamental problem. Water was flowing into the dam faster than they were letting it flow out.

This sent a shiver up and down my spine. Those poor people in the Evacuation Centre must be angry, confused, and scared. When they evacuated, their homes and possessions were likely to be damaged. The decision to open the floodgates made this a certainty.

Friday 1st February

The dam is now sitting at 190.6% capacity. You read that correctly – 190.6%!

A dam sitting above your town holding nearly twice as much as the recommended amount of water makes everyone fear the worst.

Will the wall hold?

At 11.30am, the gates transitioned to manual operation. Opening or closing the gates was no longer going to be left to a committee who programmed the gates' usage during sunny weather many years ago. Minute by minute decisions needed to be made by informed people who were on the spot.

Their decision was to open all three gates to 2.75m.

by Liz Keeley

This meant hundreds more homes would be threatened or destroyed by fast moving flood waters escaping the dam.

As the Evacuation Centres grew in number, so did the anger and fear of the tired, unwashed, hungry people and pets temporarily living within them.

Sat 2nd February

Rain is still falling.

The dam is now at 216% capacity. Meteorologists cannot accurately predict when the event will cease. At 5.30pm, the spillway gates opened another meter to 3.75m. What does this mean? Another 82 million cubic meters of water has been set free to play havoc on the people below.

To put that in perspective, that's like pulling the plug on a full MCG sized bathtub 52 times.

Doorknocking commenced to prepare residents for evacuation in the low-lying areas of Oonoonba, Idalia, Rosslea, Hermit Park, Railway Estate, South Townsville, Cluden, Townsville City and Hyde Park.

Every night, we turned on the television and watched this disaster unfold. Every night we'd see those poor people and their pets living in emergency conditions in the evacuation centres. Every night my husband and I would ask each other, "What can we do?"

And still the rain fell.

Mon 4th February

The dam is at 247.6% capacity. About 1000 people have taken refuge in Townsville's evacuation centres and more than 850 SES requests are made in 24 hours.

Torrential rain is still falling.

Tuesday 5th February

To this point, I have heard nothing but news and stories of people, families and pets being evacuated by emergency services throughout the night in flood waters. I'm sickened by this and deeply affected. But what can I do? How can one person make a difference? What can I do?

I decide to take my dog wash trailer to my closest evacuation centre and start washing some dogs. I could only imagine all those families lying on mattresses on cold floors with their pets huddled next to them and whatever small belongings they could gather.

What I saw was worse than I had imagined...

When I walked into the centre and explained to the lovely Red Cross volunteers who were organising things what I intended to do, I was immediately distracted and went speechless. The sea of vacant looks on people's faces was confronting. There were mattresses, sheets and towels strewn across the floor. A group of teenagers were hanging around a power point waiting to charge their mobile phones. The uncertainty, helplessness and fear were palpable.

The Red Cross volunteers took me to an outside covered area where people with pets were situated. I saw more rows of mattresses and animal cages, dogs tied on pieces of rope to their owners and everyone looking beaten and bedraggled. And the smell! You can only imagine the smell these poor people were enduring. It reminded me of stale swamp water that had been left sitting in the sun for too long. And that is a generous description. I can still remember the smell to this day.

The dogs were scared. Every single one of them. There were no waggy tails or happy yips. I remember

by Liz Keeley

approaching a Blue Heeler who was sitting under a chair his owner was sitting on. The poor pooch did not even get up to say "Hello" when I came over. I could almost see the sadness and fear on the dog's face. These people had all waded through flood water with their pets during torrential rain. Most had been evacuated by locals who volunteered to assist emergency services by rescuing trapped residents by boat from their flooded homes. The large number of volunteers, boats and resulting troupe of helpers were later dubbed the "tinny army" by local media.

I set up my trailer and the Red Cross volunteers went around and let everyone know they could bring their dogs outside for a free warm-water wash and blow dry.

The queue started to form...

I was shocked when I discovered most people wanted to pay me and didn't understand why I was doing it free of charge. I said, "I can't do much to help but at least you can sleep next to a clean smelling dog tonight." There were so many tears. These pet owners simply craved the idea of hugging their dogs and providing them with comfort. The simple pleasure of sleeping next to their nicely smelling dog and being looked after made such an impact on these people who have just lost so much. They needed to know others cared.

Word got out.

Wednesday 6th February

The rain has not let up and now the worst was yet to come. The Ross River running through Townsville, had received 850,000 megalitres of rainfall and the dam was at 3.8 times its capacity. They were going to have to let the flood gates open or risk the dam itself.

Dare I say, the situation was fluid and fast moving...

At 4.22pm, residents were warned the dam spillway gates may open to full setting between 8.30pm and 6.00am. Between 5.04pm - 6.06pm, repeated evacuation warnings were sent to the public regarding flood levels and the potential for dam gates to fully open. At 7.24pm, residents were warned the dam spillway gates are expected to open between 8.00pm and 8.30pm. At 8.09pm, residents were warned to evacuate as dam gates are now fully open in line with the EAP.

What followed was a flood of biblical proportions with hundreds of millions of dollars damage to property ensuing.

Thursday 7th February

I had spent the previous 2 days attending other shelters and washing people's dogs. By now though, most people were being moved on. Some went back to their homes; others were being taken in by family and friends or even strangers in the community.

Friday 8th February

The rain began to back off.

We quickly resumed normal work and had realised lots of our regular clients had taken in either friends, family or strangers and their pets. We decided to wash any extra dogs at our clients' houses at no charge while they were there.

The longest remaining person was 18 months at her friend's house. I remember the day I turned up...

My client had said her friend, her husband, 2 teenage kids and their Labrador were living with them as their house was uninhabitable. When I arrived, my client and her friend were sitting out the back having a cuppa and chatting. Both their husbands had gone back to the house to start the clean-up process and both women were quite anxious. You see, after the actual flooding, two additional deaths were reported due to melioidosis with at least 10 more hospitalised with the bacterial infection. This bacteria lives in the north Queensland soil and had made its way inside houses via floodwater. It was responsible for the condemning of many, many houses that needed to be demolished as it could not always be removed. Consequently, safety gear needed to be worn and you could not have open wounds if you were helping clean up.

After a quick discussion on how the clean-up was going, we turned out attention to the dogs. The visiting Labrador, Molly, was happily playing with the Maltese, Charlie. They were running around on the back patio playing tug with an old toy. Both dogs quickly ran up to me, Charlie, knowing it was bath day, was extra excited to see me and Molly, while cautious meeting a stranger, quickly realised there were treats in my pocket. We became fast friends!

This became an all-too-common story for all of us in our dog wash trailers. Steph, Karina, David, Jess and Jackson, who all worked with me at the time, would often tell me stories of having an extra dog (or 3) to wash at their clients' homes. We unanimously decided we would wash these visiting dogs for the duration of their stay while displaced from their homes.

So many people wanted to pay and kept asking, "Why are we doing this for free?" "Are we being paid by someone?" Our reply every time was, "We can't do much to help but at least we can wash your dog."

Sunday 17th February

The Townsville City Council learned what we had done and asked if we would organise a Council event on The Strand (our local beach strip.) We held this on Sunday 17th February, hoping to reach many more people in the community who were affected. Two of my operators, David McDonald and Jess Brodie, joined me with their trailers and we provided free washes for anyone's dogs who had been affected by the floods. Our General Manager, Christine Taylor, had been checking in with us regularly and offering assistance. When she heard what we were doing, she quickly sent up boxes of shampoo to use on the day and throughout the clean-up.

In conjunction with our local foster and rehoming groups, the Council put together donations of pet food, supplies, bedding, and blankets. We donated boxes of dog toys, new dog blankets, treats and washed over 60 dogs on the day. I remember thinking I was so very sore and tired at the end of the day. It was probably the most exhausted after working I've ever been. It was also the most fulfilled and emotional I'd ever been.

In reliving those days and talking to people, we can identify now this was our survivor guilt at work. None of us directly lost homes or loved ones, but the guilt of watching friends, family and almost half of our town go through such an emotional and physical loss impacted all of us more than we realised.

As a result, our community came together in February of 2020 as described. It was the biggest event our town had ever seen. To be phoned up and invited because of our small contribution was very emotional for myself and my team. We turned up with our trailers and chatted to many people on the day and the community response was overwhelming. People came by to say thank-you and remembered me giving their dog a free wash. Then they started asking if I was available to regularly wash their precious pooches into the future. Our business thrived through our community spirit and we were so proud to be able to help. You see, all we wanted to do was wash dogs so that they didn't smell and their owners would give them a hug.

Aftermath

I have so many stories to share of this time and the memories will stay with me forever. I wish I could put it all on paper. I must thank everyone who supported and helped during this crisis...

My husband Chris Keeley and my daughter who worried about how much I was working. My Townsville team of Steph Miller, David McDonald, Karina Denkewitz, Jess Brodie, and Jackson Collins. My Franchise Family Christine Taylor, David McNamara, Paul and Megan Walters. My dad, Albert Bonassi, for being on call to repair my trailers and my mum, Marianne Bonassi, for encouraging me to write this chapter.

Alicia James

How do you want to think? What a strange question, I hear you say. But is it? Only you should have the power to answer this question.

My chapter, *Sssh I am Not Who You Think I am* aims to be a step along the way to removing from your life the nay sayers and those who think you less than you are. These people are holding you back and too often trying to impose their way or thinking upon you.

With over a decade leading change programs, I've discovered telling people how to think generally does not bring about the positive long-term results they want. However, when you create a smorgasbord of choices aimed at facilitating active decision making and opportunities to provide answers to the many 'what's in it for me' and 'remind me why are we changing' questions, well... that's when people buy into the need to change. Beyond that, change is inevitable.

If only I'd have known all this when I needed to change all those years ago!

At ChangeITUP Change Management we use a unique approach and consider all the moving elements required to implement our *GetIT Right First* Time Change Framework. Then we work with your team to massage the change process so they feel like they own it.

If you enjoy my story about finding my voice, I'd love to learn your story. Who knows? Maybe we can help each other. My story is all about finding the courage to change and the personal growth that arises as a consequence. This is exactly what I love about my work leading change management projects in the corporate sector.

Email | info@aliciajamesofficial.com

by Alicia James

Sssh... *I am not who you think* I am.

From as far back as I can recall, this phrase has been swimming around my head. Either she is saying it to me, or I am saying it to her. You see, her perception of my lack of brightness gnaws away at my confidence which sometimes erodes my self-esteem.

Once when I was much younger, she said it as though it was an agreement we had already reached, "Alicia, you know that you are not very bright, so what you should do is to become a nurse, so that when you get married and have children you can always go back to it." The trouble with defending myself against this statement is I wanted some of it to be true! Well... I wanted kids. I wanted to get married. Yet her matter-of-fact tone and the statement itself indicated nurses are not bright and their lives are, without exception, mundane. Worse, she believes I am not capable of anything greater than this due to my lack of brightness.

Well, have I got news for her- *Sssh! I'm not who you think I am.*

I am telling you my story because it is no longer my story but her story. Yet at that time, it was very much my story and my mind-soaked IT (the voice in my head) up whenever the focus was on me.

My story is for all people, girls and boys, women, and men, who have been told you can't determine your future. It's for the people who have been told to think small so you do not get disappointed and for goodness sakes know your place! I hope this chapter helps you take the first step in not caring about IT and from now on and in this minute, you stand in plain sight in all your perceived awkwardness or ineptness and say out loud to IT, *sssh... I'm not who you think I am!*

According to my father, I was born when the sun was rising. I have always interpreted this as meaning I am all brightness – just as Simba is shown off to the animal kingdom by the Shaman, I too was destined for great things and, most assuredly, if the sun was rising in the Island of Antigua over 50 years ago in the small town of Ottos in St Johns, well, that was proof enough, all will be well in my world.

I was born to parents who were well respected in the community. My father met my mother in Antigua and once married, soon started to make a family. My parents wanted the best for their children. This desire required my father to go to the United Kingdom with my sister when she was 9 weeks old so she could be in front of the best orthopaedic surgeons. My two brothers and I remained with our mother until around two years later when my father sent for my mother, my two brothers and I to join him and my sister in the UK. A year later my younger brother was born and not long after that my youngest sister was born. The family was complete.

The brightness narrative all started at around the age of nine when I said in some ridiculous story that I could remember everything I had learnt at school. To this day, I do not know exactly why I absent mindedly said that in a conversation with my mother and father, but it was my mother who took umbrage to this ridiculous comment.

This was a triggering statement for my mother, and it became a point of honour for her to prove that in no way could this be true. So, her tests to disprove my silly statement began.

She told me to spell the word *beautiful.* I couldn't, even with the use of syllables. Bew-ti-ful. This did not help me in the slightest! A sense of quiet panic found its way in my throat making it drier than it already was. Then there was the fear of that *I-didn't-think -so* expression on her face which further sapped my self-esteem.

A series of punishments would follow incidents like these. Not physical but mental. One time, a day trip to Buckingham Palace was planned for the family. The fortunate bright siblings were allowed to go. This did not include me. Punishment and learning were frequently aligned with my West Indian culture. Yet, it's kind of a silly thinking punishment and withholding joy would create a bright mind. I mean, was missing out on a great educational outing going to result in miraculous brightness?

Consistently being told I wasn't very bright made me shyer than I already was. After all, it's not usually considered a motivational technique!

Confirmation of not been very bright began to show up predictably, in fact, right on cue... when I was asked to recite learnt bible stories from memory in front of the congregation on Sabbath mornings. No matter

by Alicia James

what I did, no sound would come out of my parched mouth and my brain drew a blank. I would try not to look at the pitying faces in the congregation looking back at me again in what seemed to be a reoccurring Sabbath morning nightmare.

Needless to say, I did not go to university as only bright people go to the places where bright ones become brighter. Instead, I threw myself into reading to gain knowledge. I started to read self-help books to give me the confidence I so wanted and needed to begin to live outside of my head. I also started to focus on what I knew for certain I had. You see, when I could muster it, so many had complimented me on it that I believed it to be true. I had a good speaking voice.

A good speaking voice was very much encouraged and very important to both parents. Being able to speak well was a very big deal and I was able to capitalise on something that came easily to me. In time, I learned to use it to get through many interviews and for getting people to take notice of me.

IT started to show up less and less as I did not encounter *IT* when I did what I wanted to do, or so I thought. As time went on, I worked in various temporary roles which I landed based on the sound of my voice. For example, front of office or receptionist roles were easy enough for me to get due to my voice. Any initial nerves gradually disappeared. So, feeling the fear, which is what *IT* was and still is, and doing what scares the living daylights out of you anyway became my motto. *Feel the fear and do it anyway.* Positive self-talk is not at all new and even with the positive self-talk, it sometimes is hard to disassociate yourself from the fear and retain what you want to speak on with confidence. But you need to start somewhere, and you need to let *your* demon know who the boss is.

I started to acknowledge my fears to myself... yes, I feared speaking, but life kept me in roles that would keep me speaking often and a lot. One of my earliest roles was in the recruitment industry where the job was mostly selling why, as a recruiter, we had the best applicants for the job to the client. Additionally, we had to persuade applicants that we had just the right contract for them, and I found that I was really good at doing this, matching clients with the right candidate and matching candidates with the right contract, this was called a placement and I got these placements on a weekly basis and always ready to start work on Monday.

I knew that I was going to be exceptional at something and I wanted it to be more than I was at the time – I did not know what, but I did know that I wanted more.

The years rolled by. On a holiday in Australia, I met my now ex-husband and the-recruiter-who-always-had-a-starter-for-Monday could not transition that skill set to the Australian Market.

I moved to other roles and eventually entered the public service as a trainer. This was a pivotal time for me as the project I was involved in was due for evaluation. The result of that project evaluation? There were too many trainers on the project! So, I was moved into a change analyst role with no experience and no understanding of what the role involved or required me of me.

For the longest while, I felt like a fish out of water. I felt like I was thrashing around in a dry bucket that was labelled with Imposter Syndrome. So, guess who reaffirmed my not very brightness. Guess who initiated the doubt. Guess whose criticisms raced around my head.

by Alicia James

I did not logically believe I was not bright. But when you are told this at an impressionable age, you tend to initially work with the hand you are dealt. I did, and on a superficial level felt it to be true as I was pretending to be what I was not. Because let's face it, at that time... I was not a change analyst!

To silence the voice, I attended a short course in change management based on implementing change. That course changed my career path as so many pieces fell into place. I finally made sense of what I wanted to do. It became clear why I liked working the way I did and tackling problems was one of my specialties.

I also realised, I have a combination of good gut sense, was good at unpacking problems and my approach to solving problems was repeatable. The 3-day course opened a career opportunity but I wanted more. I soon left the permanency of the public service and entered the contract market as an Organisational Change Manager predominantly in government departments.

I am sure that you can recognise the patten here. Change Management requires you to engage with an inexhaustive range of stakeholder groups and address them in large numbers. So why did I continue to feel the public speaking nerves that kept me focused on what I needed to say next instead of just telling a good story?

My quest to be considered bright and accepted in a field that I was already competent in took me down the study path. At this time, I wanted to be believable as a change manager and a qualification in a school for brightness would prove that. I graduated with a certificate in change management at the UNSW in

2016. I was beyond thrilled to be *qualified* to speak on change management topics and could confidently demonstrate my knowledge in interviews where I was often shortlisted if not successful in landing the role.

I wanted to do more with my experience and remembered going back to a government department where, in a project meeting, I found my voice and decided to speak up. It was the first opportunity to comment on a project that I was assigned to and did so with only the slightest hesitation. I deliberately made eye contact with individuals around the meeting table and as I spoke and drew every one of them into what I was saying. I felt powerful and knowledgeable.

I often wish my mother was around to see what I have achieved over the years. My 12-year marriage gave me the joy of my life, my now 24-year-old son who is a smart, witty, intelligent, and a downright funny young man. He is the product of my instilling in him, he can achieve anything he wants to do achieve and above all, he should live the life he is meant to.

2021 was a year where everything happened at once and I am saying to myself, why not me? Why should I not speak up and own the right to speak on things that I feel strongly about. To be part of a group of writers in this anthology of chapters is a defining step in eliminating self-doubt. It is part of my transition to telling IT, *sssh...I'm not who you think I am* and would have made my mother question her earlier thinking about me, her daughter.

I have been invited to speak at the Festival of Business Analysis in 2022. I am so excited. To think, the girl who was once without a voice has now been offered a stage. This is extraordinary to me. So, I say to those of you who feel that what's going on in your heads is often nowhere near the truth about yourself, grab the courage, even if you do not always feel it in the moment, and tell that voice in your head, "*Sssh... I'm not who you think I am!*"

Dedication : I dedicate this chapter to my son Maxwell

Leesa Tongoulidis

Founder of Human Art Pty Ltd - Leesa specialises in helping people navigate uncertainty and change. Using design thinking, heart-based leadership practices and innovative people strategies, Leesa purpose is to change the way we think and feel about our work.

Leesa has amassed over three decades of experience in executive, leadership, HR, and front line sales roles, spanning multiple operating circumstances and industry sectors. These include Health, Engineering, IT, Financial Services, Utilities, Government, Education and Telecommunications.

Leesa is a lateral thinker, and a visionary. Her commercial acumen and curiosity coupled with her ability to flex and adapt to fluid situations has given her the opportunity to learn from and work with the best in her field. She is pragmatic, down to earth, a fun, creative and empathic leader who delights in seeing others succeed and grow.

Volatility, uncertainty, complexity and ambiguity are here to stay, meaning we all need to show up differently, cultivate new ways of working, learn (and unlearn) new skills and capabilities, adopt more conscious leadership practices and whole brain thinking. Leesa uses the lens of an artist, as both a metaphor and catalyst for deep reflective change and personal growth. Her own experiences with mental illness and recovery offer clients a unique and trauma-informed perspective on ways to approach and co-create positive change.

Leesa is an experienced speaker, strategist, coach, facilitator, and enjoys mentoring and supporting young adults, refugees, women. She is on a mission to help them find their voice and step forward into a better future.

Email	leesa@humanart.com.au
LinkedIn, Personal	linkedin.com/in/leesatongoulidis
Facebook	facebook.com/leesa.tongoulidis.7
Twitter	twitter.com/LTongoulidis
Email, Business	leesa@humanart.com.au
Website, Business	humanart.com.au
LinkedIn, Business	linkedin.com/company/humanartcareerandleadershipcoaching

by Leesa Tongoulidis

The unfinished **Artist**

"We have to find our heart songs all by ourselves
It's the voice you hear inside.
Who you truly are."

Song of the Heart, Happy Feet - Prince

Layer upon layer, the emotional armor many of us manage to accumulate over our lifetimes can get pretty, damn heavy. Knowing or unknowingly, some stay locked in that armor their entire lives, never reaching their full potential, never realising their dreams. Too disturbed, too distressed, unable to seek or access the right support to help them navigate a way out. Too scared or perhaps ashamed to seek help, they simply cannot find a way out of the maze.

I didn't know I was in the maze.

Where there is smoke...

by Leesa Tongoulidis

January 2020. The NSW bushfires were raging, lives were being lost, homes and businesses were reduced to rubble and ashes. Animals were dying and huge amounts of bushland were left charred and smoking. It felt like Armageddon. Even though I was safe and sound in my own home in Sydney, I was very distressed just witnessing all the carnage unfolding. Heavy smoke filled the air. The heat felt inescapable. My heart was hurting for everyone who was suffering. With a barrage of chronic immune system disorders, including asthma, I was holed up at home during this time with the air purifier choking so I didn't. I was out of work and frustrated about applying for jobs, getting to and from various job interviews, avoiding all the smoke and getting more anxious by the minute. In the previous two years, I had undergone surgeries for two separate knee replacements. I hate to admit it, but I had been living silently in pain for many, many years.

When my role became redundant a few months earlier, I thought I was ok with it. After all, I had been through this type of thing before. I told myself it was no big deal. I had the support of my husband and my family who were very caring and understanding. I was in a good place, relatively speaking. I knew things would eventually work themselves out.

My body had other plans.

Without any warning, and in the space of a week of losing my job, I had two trips to St Vincent's Hospital emergency department with blood pressure readings at 250+/150 and erratic heart palpitations. My head was calm, but my body was not. I had experienced this once before. My mind started to tick. What was going on with my body? I had to find out. This was serious. It could be a matter of life or death. How could I be so stupid? How could I be so ignorant of my own health needs? In the middle of my turmoil, my cardiologist and neurologist suggested I see a psychologist.

After a few weeks. things settled down. I went away with my husband on a wonderful, relaxing and much needed holiday to Bali. We were celebrating our 25th Wedding Anniversary. The psychologist appointment would just have to wait.

Did I really want to go and see the psychologist? No... not really. But, I thought I should do the right thing and follow the advice I was given, there was obviously something there that needed to be explored. I reluctantly made that first call a few weeks after I came back from my holiday. To be honest, I didn't know what to expect but my sense was that many of my chronic and episodic health issues were linked in some way to my dysfunctional family life as a kid. I couldn't be sure. I thought I had processed all of that, and before moved on.

Maybe I hadn't?

My mum smoked all the way through her pregnancies, dad was a smoker and a functioning alcoholic. I lived in Cabramatta, in the heart of the western suburbs of Sydney. We were surrounded by housing commission homes and many families who were also struggling in one way or another. My grandfather had built our house and my dad owned a business, so I felt we were better off than most. Domestic violence and substance abuse was rife in our neighbourhood at that time.

Once I mustered the courage to attend that first meeting with the psychologist, I became curious and decided it was time to open my mind. I was ready to face the process, come what may. A few weeks in, lots of tears later, I was diagnosed with Complex Post

Traumatic Stress Disorder or CPTSD. My first reaction of course was denial. I felt enormous shame and guilt.

Finally, the penny dropped and things started clicking into place. I was beating myself and my inner child up for not being good enough, not being strong enough. My denial phase went on for several months. I then started reading Bessel van der Kolk MD's book – The Body Keeps the Score. What a revelation!

Whilst I was relieved in many ways to finally have some answers, I really needed to sit with this news and metabolise it. Sitting quietly in the corner of our living room, nothing could have prepared me for the state of shock I was about to enter as I continued to turn the pages and read on. I didn't say a word to anyone. Everything, I mean *everything* I was reading was spot on. I felt myself being triggered at every possible level. Had I been living under a rock all my life? van der Kolk had me to a tee. How could I have not known? How could it have slipped by others? Had I been in denial my entire life? I was full of questions, anger, explosive rage and uncontrollable grief. I had nowhere to point all that energy. So, I went inwards, just like I always did. At that moment, I felt like my life had been an absolute sham. I was quickly sliding into a severe disassociated mental state. Everything I said was complete gibberish and made no sense at all. I felt like I was speaking inside a dream, in a secret code almost. My husband and daughters, were all deeply distressed. Yep, it was time to go to the hospital… again!

I won't go into all the details but suffice to say the image of Linda Blair's head spinning around in the movie, The Exorcist seems fitting. I was in a state of psychosis, had suffered a stroke and pneumonia, courtesy of the bushfires, a rare type of heart failure called Tako-Subo (broken heart syndrome) and unusual heart arrythmia, that I have had all my life apparently. What the %$#@? In hindsight, I realised that I probably didn't pick a good time to confront my diagnosis. How was I to know that the suffering I had experienced so long ago would resurface now and manifest in this way.

A Mother's love...

My mum was a strong and loving influence in my life. She shaped many of my beliefs, my outlook on life and expectations for the future. She was part of the very aptly named "silent generation." She was extremely hard on herself and carried more pain and shame than I could possibly ever imagine having in my own life. I lived and learnt about life from the shadows of her trauma. She had a wicked sense of humour, which I thankfully inherited. She always tried to make light of whatever was going on at home. I think the movie Life is Beautiful sums up the lengths she would go to, to take care of her children.

On the bad days, she would sit there in silence and just take the abuse and vitriole, the gaslighting, the psychological torments, the lies. As a young child I remember sitting gently and calmly beside her, holding her hand. She had nowhere to go, no family, no escape.

She lost her own mum at the age of 7. A single gunshot to the head. Her father told the police, it was suicide. Mum never knew the truth until much, much later. That truth? Her father had been convicted of murder. The family was split up and she was sent to live in an orphanage with her sister in the country. No explanation, no information. She lived there for the next seven years and was subjected to all types of physical abuse and cruelty at the hands of the Catholic Church. Her younger brother was sent off to a different orphanage, where he also suffered cruelty and sexual abuse. Her older sister went to live with relatives. My grandfather was, according to the court transcripts, mysteriously pardoned and ended up in Europe serving in the armed services in the Second World War. When he returned home, he went back to his cruel ways. Abusing and sexually assaulting each of his daughters on more than one occasion. They were too scared and frightened to say anything. Things like that were swept under the carpet in those times. Women and children had no voice, no recourse.

My own dad was slightly better. He never physically hurt me, but he did push my mum around. Despite knowing her past. My Mum did not deserve this type of life. I was devasted, disgusted, terrified. This just couldn't be allowed to keep happening, but it did. I think I lost my own identity and sense of self without even realising it. I knew deep down that if anything happened to mum, things were not going work out well for me or my siblings. I felt I had no other choice... it was literally a matter of life or death, maybe something even worse. I had no idea. It would have been too dangerous to back chat or confront my dad. There was no one to talk to. He stood at 6 ft 4 and when he was drunk, which was most nights, he would fly into fits of uncontrollable rage. I said nothing.

Every day was a blame game of one sort or another. My dad rarely took any interest in what I had to say, or what I did. Every now and then he would surprise me, by seeming interested. It was always short lived.

The wonder years...

Lucky me! I scored a job straight out of school as a trainee bank clerk. I was sixteen, very naïve and looked like a Lady Di impersonator when I showed up for my first day. Hair flicks, drop waisted dress, peter pan collar and all. I loved the independence and the pay ($90 a week – woo hoo!) My goal was to learn everything I could, look after my mum and make a new life. I had stepped onto my magic carpet, there was no going back. I had finally escaped.

I went on to experience some further harrowing and traumatic experiences, including two armed bank robberies, sexual assault, gun violence and including quite a few cases of innappropriate workplace behaviour. Although nothing was as bad as living through years of domestic abuse and extreme family dysfunction. Such is life, I thought...suck it up, hope for better times ahead.

By the age of 21, I had met my would-be husband and decided I had to knuckle down and make a proper future for myself. I enrolled in a Diploma of Human Resources at TAFE, saved a deposit and bought a unit. It was more than I could have ever dreamt of achieving in life at the time. I was filled with pride for what I had accomplished at such a young age. My husband was and continues to be my rock. He has been by far my biggest supporter and the reason I continue to persevere in making every day better than the last.

I worked hard, got promoted, went on to lead some amazing change and transformation projects, work with some fantastic people and organisations. I was having the time of my life. I knew on some level, that each one of my successes was a thorn in my father's side, he never acknowledged any of them.

A few years later, I got married, bought a house, gave birth to two incredible daughters, now in their twenties, who are doing great things with their lives. I was determined, never to repeat any of the patterns of the past with my own family. I was on a mission and I was unstoppable.

On the outside at least, everything looked good.

When I returned to the workforce and found myself with family and eldercare responsibilities, I experienced work from a different perspective. I became acutely aware of and experienced first-hand discrimination on multiple levels. My future career path emerged all of those experiences and my focus shifted into Organisational Development, Inclusion, Diversity, Leadership and Talent Management. I was driven towards roles that improve organisational culture and employee engagement, the types of issues that afflict so many businesses today. The past and the future were coming together in unusual ways for me. I hadn't expected it but I was ready all the same. I was determined to make a difference, one way or another. I would not allow myself to remain silent on these types of issues anymore. I had a voice and I was going to use it.

I came to realise that I had never actually allowed myself time to grieve my losses or acknowledge my emotional pain. Just like my mum, I had learned to suppress those feelings by throwing myself into my family, my work and everyone else. I didn't know any better.

Lighting up my own life...

Everything that I have been through has been instrumental in shaping my career, life choices including the decision to set up my own coaching and consulting business six years ago. It hasn't been easy, but then again, life very rarely ever is, for any of us.

My love of all things arty and natural creativity continues to grow and develop every day. I am now truly honouring my strengths, my values and innate talents. My curiosity and interests in behavioural science and emergent leadership practice have been instrumental in accelerating my healing process, but I know now, that the work never stops, when it comes to healing from trauma.

My eyes are fully open and I have learned to reframe my past and weave my experiences, my research and knowledge into my work. I truly believe that there is enormous value to be tapped into by leveraging more neuro-diverse views in reshaping the way our systems, government, society and organisations operate.

Whilst I have always been able to navigate complexity and uncertainty with grace and care, I now do it with more compassion for myself. The challenges of Covid, everything else of course add another whole layer of complexity of what comes next for all of us.

It is my sincere hope that by reading my story, you give yourself the space to reflect and bring more light into your own life. I hope that it encourages you to share more of who you really are with the world and those around you.

Dedication : I dedicate this chapter to my friend Sara, who inspires me every day.

"To show the world how perfect we were, my mother would send us across the road and, using hand signals, we had to let her know when the curtains were balanced so everyone saw only perfection within what we knew to be our four prison walls."

Jenni Tarrant

Jenni Tarrant

Jenni Tarrant is a highly successful business-woman in the Australian hairdressing industry, and so much more. She is equally driven to ease the burdens, and enhance the physical and psychological well-being of vulnerable people in our community.

Over her 52 years, life has thrown Jenni challenges that may have broken the spirit of many others. Hers is a success story of thriving despite adversity in her personal life and career. She describes herself as determined, sometimes to the point of bloody-minded, which is key to her achieving each of her lofty goals and then surging on to the next one.

Like women the world over, Jenni juggles her many roles as a wife, mother, and friend, with being a business owner, leader, and philanthropist. She expects the very best of herself, and mentors others who ask her to help them do the same.

Jenni was a quiet achiever until relatively recently when people encouraged her to put herself forward and nominated her for awards. Since that time, Jenni has won national awards for business success, customer care, training, sustainability, and humanitarian efforts, to name a few. She recently received an Order of Australian Medal from the Governor-General for her contribution to the Australian hairdressing industry and humanitarian efforts.

Email	bhr@bondhairreligion.com
LinkedIn	linkedin.com/in/jennitarrant
Bus 1. Website	bondhairreligion.com
Bus 1. Instagram	@houseofbond
Bus 1. Facebook	facebook.com/bondhairreligionkingston
Bus 2. Website	bondbody.com. au
Bus 2. Instagram	@bondbodyandbrowbar

by Jenni Tarrant

Fight to **Flight**

What happened to my shell didn't matter as long as I protected that beautiful, little blond girl who laughed and danced in a field of white daisies.

We spend our childhoods learning how to be the adults of our futures with the guidance of those around us to mould us and show us wrong and right, love and hate. For me, childhood was a mixture of fear, shame, guilt and pain.

My mother struggled with dark demons that shaped her world into one of torment. Out of this rose a profound anger that manifested in screaming for hours on end, violent outbursts, slapping and punching and a deep desire for constant cleaning and perfection inside our home. My younger sister and I lived in constant fear of physical and mental abuse.

School was the only time away from our home. We were never allowed to play with other children after school or ride bikes or invite friends home. So I spent time watching others through the window of our perfect house that was filled with fear.

During school holidays, I was able to have a break from my mother's constant cleaning and screaming and abuse as my sister and I were taken away by someone known to our family for the break. But... it wasn't much of a break.

In their place, I was repeatedly raped by this person and their friends. Then I would be returned to sender when the holidays were done. And there was no one to tell the truth to. It filled me with shame, fear, confusion and guilt. How could I be such a terrible child to make these people do what they did to me? What made me so horrible?

Once back home, my mother's abuse was like a branding iron as soon as I walked in the door. My shoes had to be polished to a mirror finish. My bed had to be made to a specific measurement. I had to be dressed perfectly. My hair was pulled so tight on my head into the perfect bun. Then I was told to smile so the world would see the pretty girl with the perfect family.

To show the world how perfect we were, my mother would send us across the road and, using hand signals, we had to let her know when the curtains were balanced so everyone saw only perfection within what we knew to be our four prison walls.

This was my life until I was 13. Then one average day my life changed when my mother took me with her to a hairdressing salon. As a very tall, very withdrawn, incredibly shy young girl with very little self-esteem, I looked around to see a group of people laughing, creating and clearly loving what they did. I am unsure where the courage came from, but I walked across to the owner and asked, "Do you need anyone to help on Saturdays?" I left my phone number and within a couple of weeks I was contacted and asked to come in for a trial. That was the day my chosen career saved my life. You see, due to working the late nights, Saturdays and full-time during school holidays, I could no longer go away with the people who were my sexual abusers. Though the abuse had ceased, the enduring physical and mental trauma of those 10 years was still rooted in my soul.

During this time, home was becoming more and more threatening as my mother's rage was becoming more and more out of control. It's unclear to me when I decided to become the protector of my younger sister and my father, but I did. Watching them live in fear was intolerable and if my abusers mistreated me then I'd either be protecting my sister from the sexual abuse or my dad and sister from the beatings. I have an enduring image of taking the pure, little girl who lived deep within me and putting her in box before wrapping chains around that box. What happened to my shell didn't matter as long as I protected that beautiful, little blond girl who laughed and danced in a field of white daisies. Knowing she was safe meant nothing could touch me or hurt me and the world could see the pretty, compliant, people-pleasing girl that everyone needed to see. Then the shame and pain could be pushed down into a dark place that only I knew and the world never saw.

This need to protect others helped me survive. At that young age, it can only have come from instinct. I'm so lucky as this instinct gave me purpose, courage and a willingness to go through the pain again and again.

From the age of 14, hairdressing gave me a space to be who I wanted to be. No one knew my shame, no one knew my pain, no one had heard me scream. However, one of the lasting scars to that point was my shyness and this caused problems within the early years of my by Jenni Tarrant

career. You see, speaking up after so many years of being told not to, and being made to feel like I didn't have a voice, and "no one would believe you anyway" made it very difficult for me. Nonetheless, I had other desirable traits. Thanks to my mother... I could clean like crazy woman! Finally, a talent was being praised.

During this time, I was living for work. It was my escape and even on the hard days it was nothing compared to the life I had endured and still faced. The pretty girl with the perfect home and family was how the world saw me and that was the lie I was still telling myself and others.

At 16, my mother went to hit me once again and something snapped inside me. No more would I be a punching bag. No more would I be belittled. No more would I accumulate the shame. No more. I struck back. I hit her. I yelled at her. That day a courage came from a place unknown to me. That day was the fork in the road. That day, I tried to overdose. That day, after wanting to leave this world so many times I felt more ashamed than I ever had before. That day, I was ashamed because I had become her.

So many years of pain. So much guilt and sorrow and rage and hurt. It was too much for one little girl. I needed a break from it. I needed to hide. I wanted to hug my little daisy-dancing self but she was getting further away.

Fortunately for me, medication wasn't very prevalent in our house and what I had taken only made me sick and drowsy. The effect of that day had shaken my parents. I am unaware if that was the day mum decided to seek psychiatric help or not, but this happened soon after and her journey down this path was long and incredibly difficult as her demons were deep, dark and painful. A few years later, I sadly discovered her childhood paralleled my own. What do they say about the apple and the tree?

I won't say the following years were perfect. As with many things in life, it takes time to unlearn patterns of anger and letting go of unhealthy control. Yet I did get to see more joy in our home, more laughter and less fear. I grew to see the kindness and beauty in my mum, I got to watch my parent's relationship evolve. My sister and I slowly began to feel safe, like kids should.

I have been asked many times how I survived when so many don't. After many years of thinking about this, I believe, even in the darkest moments, there were still times that I felt loved by both of my parents. At the core there was love and this got me through. Today, mum and I have a wonderful relationship. She is everything I could have ever wished for and even though forgiveness is not easy, it is the only way forward to have the life you dream of.

My hairdressing career forged ahead. My passion and love for my craft only became greater as I completed my apprenticeship in the very same salon I started in at 14.

By 19, I started to date my now husband of 33 years, Stewart. This was another turning point for me. He was my first consenting sexual partner and we progressed through our very new and wonderful relationship feeling safe, deeply loved and protected. Then, like snippets of flickering film, horrifying memories crept out of the archives. These memories left me feeling disgusting, fearful and tormented. I was very proud of being a virgin at 19 and was very strong in my belief that I would only give that part of myself to someone I loved. So I was extraordinarily confused by the feelings and memories that were invading my mind as Stewart and I progressed very slowly with this most intimate part of our relationship. What was wrong with me? Where did these film noir movies in my mind come from and why did I feel this way?

Trauma amnesia is caused when the events of the past are so terrifying the brain locks them in a cave because they are too profoundly painful. But of course, present day activities can undo the lock allowing some memories to escape.

This was me at 19. My body and mind had no memory of the sexual abuse. I had trauma amnesia but the memory leakage was catching up with me.

Whilst the outside world saw a happy, hardworking, career orientated young women with a partner who was incredibly loving, kind and patient the inner turmoil for me was overwhelming. I found myself deeply depressed, suicidal thoughts became a constant part of my everyday. I thought I was disturbed because of the visions. Crying and pain were a constant part of our lovemaking making Stewart doubt what was going wrong and in fear of touching me.

One very nondescript day, I was sitting with my sister discussing something we had seen on a talk show and I decided to share my feelings with her. Unbelievably, her reaction was one I was not expecting at all. "Me too," she said. After many hours of discussion, we both realised our visions and feelings were the same.

That was when I decided to venture into the world of personal development to study everything I could about emotions, understanding the human brain and working on putting all the puzzle pieces together. Over many years, I did everything from meditation, anger workshops, rebirthing, becoming an NLP practitioner, breath work, firewalking, trained in hypnosis and became a Lifeline counsellor... you name it, I did it.

Slowly, the memories became clear until I had all the information I needed to remember what had happened to me. To this day, I still don't remember everything and nor do I want to. I have been diagnosed with chronic PTSD, depression and anxiety. With the help of medication and my continuing desire to work on myself, I strive to move forward a little every day.

After 29 years in the hairdressing industry, I was asked by my then boss if I would like to buy the salon she had owned for 16 years. With a lot of fear, as I was still quite insecure and quiet, I decided to take on her business. What an incredible learning experience it has been. I have had incredible success and massive highs. I have been heartbroken and felt the lowest of lows. Once again, I had to face people that took from me endlessly, undermined me, went out of their way to hurt me. I felt unheard and manipulated. The things I had faced in my early life once again haunted me within my business. I chose to continue to be the people-pleaser, giving at all costs. Due to my lack of self-love, I attracted team members that went about creating the very same environment I tried so hard to run from. 17 years later, I have realised it was all part of my learning to become a leader.

Today my employees are an incredible team of passionate, creative and hardworking professionals. I have realised for me to find true happiness in my day-to-day, I had to release my little girl back into the daisies. The shell I had created was not allowing my true dreams to shine through. I needed to be vulnerable, I needed to play, I needed to dance in the daisies to find my true self and the essence of what I was trying to achieve in my home away from home. I no longer had to be the protector, I no longer had to live in fear, I no longer gave anyone the right to have control. This has taken a very long time.

At 52, I own 3 businesses. We are multi-award winning within the beauty industry and in the broader community for business, training, environmental initiatives and humanitarian endeavours.

I truly am thankful to all those who have come and gone through my businesses and the 26 who remain. I have cried a lot and learnt a lot. I have laughed more than I ever have and the doubt and fear have been replaced by a strength and determination to achieve whatever I put my mind to.

A massive part of my life has become giving to those in need. Eight years ago, with my businesses running well and my son (16 at the time) not needing me as much, I realised that raising money and awareness around childhood sexual abuse, family violence and standing up loudly for the most vulnerable was my next calling. Using our profile within the industry and my business, I embarked on a series of journeys so out of my comfort zone that people felt compelled to donate. My first fundraiser was to do Kokoda in 5 days, this for a woman that hadn't hiked in her life and, let's face it, would prefer a glass of champagne at a fashion show over not showering for 5 days! This challenge once again saw me fighting physically and mentally to finish the most difficult and exhausting thing I had ever done. Since then, I have climbed 6,000 metres above sea level to the peak of Mt Kilimanjaro. I've ridden a horse across Mongolia (I am petrified of horses!) I've lived in my Holden Barina for 7 nights in the middle of winter with it getting down to -7 degrees overnight. I've worn tape over my mouth for a week unable to speak for the silence around mental health. These are just a few of the ways we have raised money. Blanket drives, new toys for Christmas, food collections and many more are on the list. The greatest gift I could ever truly receive is the opportunity to give.

Each and every day when I wake up, I am thankful for my beautiful family. When I walk into the salon to work with my team, I am thankful for the community we have built. I am thankful for my life, my learnings, my growth and my journey that is yet to come. I have a special gratitude for my daisy-dancing little girl that shows me joy, peace, love and how to let go. And I am thankful for those that have held me up as I fell and those that held out a hand and never let go. I am excited for the learnings that are to come and the joy of life.

Other books *in the series*

RAW ~ Real Stories from Nine Resilient Women

Shame, Guilt, Ridicule, Poverty, Horror, Impotence, Violence, Fear. Nevertheless, it seems we get an (un)healthy dose of those sometimes too. Mostly, it's not a case of if… it's when. And while you can surround yourself with positive and like-minded people to help you through, when all is said and done, it's those lonely hours between 2am and 4am when we often find ourselves facing our demons.

RAW explores the trials of nine everyday women who chose to carry on. Sure, there's some baggage… but that's a hell of a lot healthier than being continuously beaten up by those demons.

Feeling like it's all about you? It's not. Take comfort from the stories of others who've walked a few miles on some windy, rocky roads through their own barren wastelands…

…and emerged stronger, sharper and ready to get on with it.

Need a new perspective? RAW may help set you on a happier path.

Get your copy now businessinheels.net/raw-book

Rise Above ~ beyond ordinary

These are eight remarkable women

Each has a story to tell

Each has a message of hope to share

This collection of stories show the might and power of eight women who refuse to be beaten. Together, they have endured hardship, broken marriages, health crises, catastrophes, self-doubt, parental discouragement, business failure and more.

Yet with grit and determination and fire in their bellies, they have forged on and rebuit their lives,businesses and careers. Their courage, resilience and deep sense of purpose has enabled each to find her path.

Get your copy now businessinheels.net/riseabove-book-order